REMO WENT ROGUE

Remo Cobb # 1

MIKE MCCRARY

A word from the Author

Remo Went Rouge was written to be a pulpy, crime novel. It's violent, completely politically incorrect and filled with enough profanity and inappropriate behavior to make a drunken sailor blush. It's a fast, crazy read and was designed to be such. It's all meant in good fun, of course, and not to be taken too seriously. If none of this sounds like your brand of vodka, then please do not pick up this book.

It's okay, really, I won't be offended. We're cool.

But if this sounds kinda fun, then please grab a copy and enjoy. I hope you do. I had a blast writing it.

Peace and love, good people.

Mike McCrary

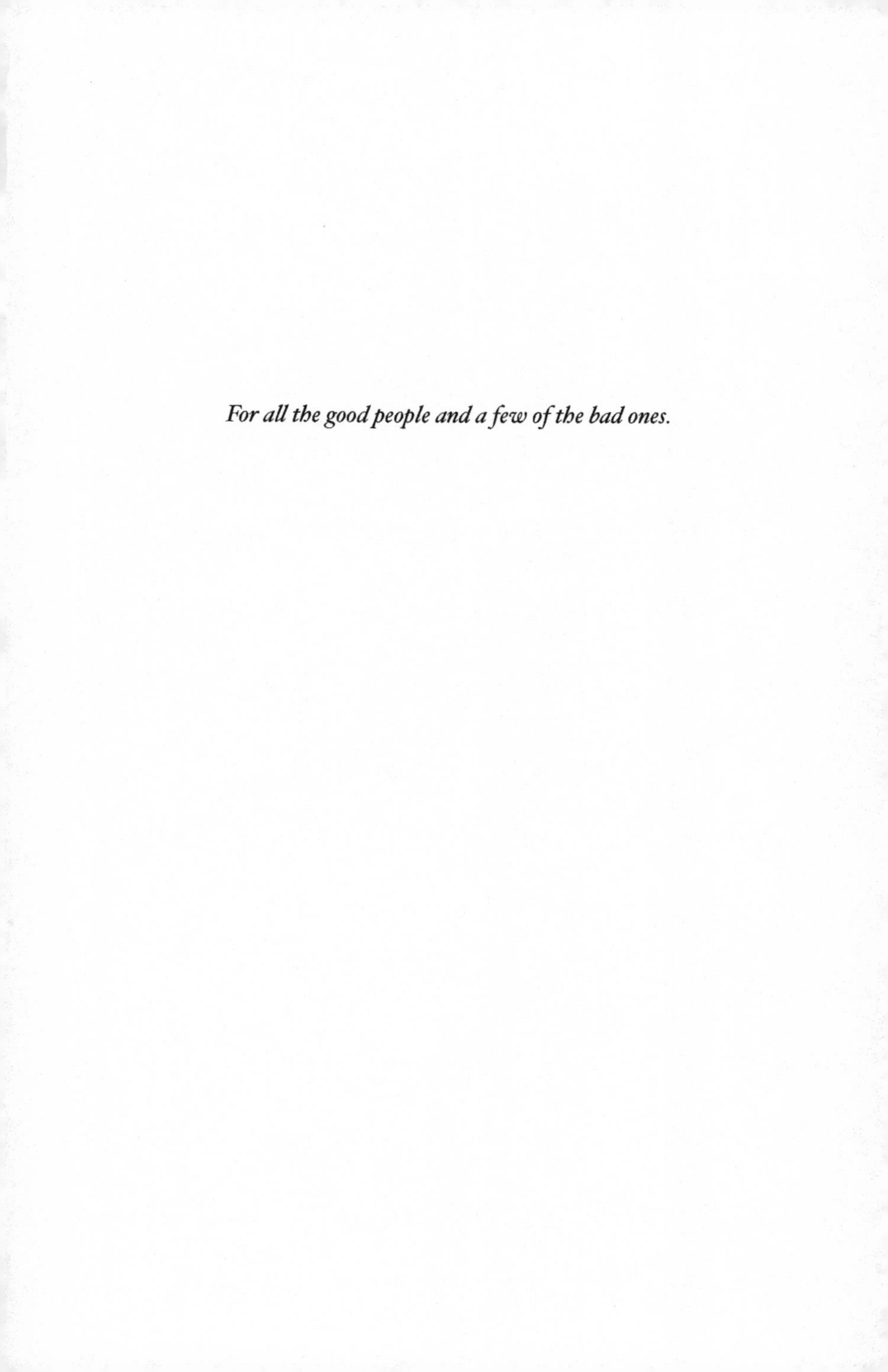

For all the good people and a few of the bad ones.

SUCH AN ASSHOLE

PART I

CHAPTER ONE

LESLIE LIKES TO FUCK MEN. Sometimes she ends up bedding some dudes that she doesn't really like. It happens.

So what?

When you're a thirty-three-year old woman living in New York and you like to fuck men, you may find yourself bedding a few pricks. Yes, the literal nature of that statement is understood, but you get it. An attractive woman in a demanding job, working ridiculous hours, surrounded by men of loose moral fiber may have to drop her standards in order to get some.

Sex or the high road. The low road has an impressive win/loss record. Again, it happens. All of this swirls around Leslie's pretty little head as she nudges back and forth on her back. On a desk. In the dark. Having sex with one of those previously-mentioned pricks.

It's not so much that Remo is a prick, really. Actually, she doesn't even know him all that well. Probably best. What she does know is that he talks while doing the deed.

Like, a lot. He's been rambling practically the whole time. With hump-altered speech, Remo tells a story. "There's this pack of vicious assholes who decide to hit a bank on a random Tuesday..."

Remo describes a seemingly normal weekday morning in the big city. Every day New Yorkers file into a Midtown bank as it opens. Good folk enter before work, grab some cash, make a deposit, bitch about a fee. All walks of life. Men, women, kids. The wealthy, the middle-class, the just-getting-by. A cultural and financial melting pot. None of them have a clue what's coming.

A van sits parked across the street. Six men wait inside the van, dressed for bad things. Armed and ready.

Three of them are the Mashburn brothers. They sit along one side. Dutch, the oldest brother, is both experienced and damned evil. The middle Mashburn is Ferris, a sharp-minded, ice shard of a man. The youngest, a wiry wacko called Chicken Wing.

On the opposite side of the creepy rape van sit two more members of this crew. Garden-variety crime boys. A slick criminal called Bobby Balls, and a young punk of a bastard called Country.

Their real names escape Remo at the moment. The final crew member is the driver, Lester, an aging career criminal who's never moved up in the ranks. Lester looks uneasy.

Uncertain. Uncomfortable. Dutch, the obvious leader, gives the nod. Dutch has his craft down, and has developed some simple rules for working jobs.

Rule # 1: He sees no reason to get creative with dead president masks or all that movie horseshit. Be nondescript; don't give the law something exotic to look into. Hmmm, where do you find this unique, hard-to-find mask? Run a check on all retailers that might carry masks like it, pull the security camera video and sync it with the register on the date those masks were sold. Any shit-stain who caught five minutes of any of the ten *Law & Order* episodes last night could piece that together. Just use something to cover your fucking face.

The crew pulls down classic black ski masks.

Rule #2: Don't use semi-automatics when doing banks. Don't

use a weapon that spits out evidence like a PEZ dispenser. All those shell casings bouncing off the floor looks fuckin' cool in the movies. Glocks going crazy, lead flying in slow-mo...but in the real world—Dutch's world—it only creates evidence for cops to bag and help them tell a story.

.357s don't leave casings.

You say, "But what if you need more bullets? You have to reload, Old West style." If you need more than five guys with seven rounds a piece to do a bank you don't deserve the take. Go suck a dick. Now if the cops join the party, that's different. The AKs on their backs are for that.

Rule #3: In case of emergency, use AK. The crew readies the guns. All nickel plated, rubber-gripped .357 magnums. AKs strapped on their backs.

And, oh yeah, Rule #4: Witnesses are like shell casings. They should not be able to help tell a story.

The van doors bust open and the masked crew pours out, armed to the teeth. One throws an innocent bystander to the concrete en route to the bank door.

The five men rage into the bank like cowboys from hell.

A relentless rat-tat popping of gunfire echoes from inside the bank. Screams wail behind the closed doors. People on the street scatter in every direction.

Lester watches from behind the wheel. His eyes drop, each pop of gunfire seeming like it physically hurts him. He rubs a small cross hanging around his neck. He hates all of this, and he doesn't even know why. He's struggling with this. It's not like he's never been around killing or killed anybody before. God knows that's not the case. But today for some reason the pounding blasts from inside the bank, the obvious outcome from those blasts, are almost too much for Lester to bear.

A final bone-rattling shot sounds from inside the bank.

Remo powers on with his mid-sex tale: "Sixteen dead. Three point two million gone. Over in two minutes and eleven seconds."

At some farmland just north of Where-the-Hell-Are-We U.S.A, the bank crew digs a massive hole to stash the cash. Large money bags drop in. Dirt falls. Another thought from Dutch, possibly Rule #5: *Don't get caught with the money.* This isn't an international crime crew of sex symbols off the lot at Warner Brothers. They don't evade laser sensors and they don't have the capacity to launder that kind of green within a day of stealing it. They need to keep it safe until the heat subsides a bit. The first forty-eight hours are dicey, but after a few days you can get your money and get on with your life. If you get pinched holding bags of money, well, your options are somewhat limited.

The crew holes up in a tiny dump of a cabin in the New Mexico mountains, living like the fucking Amish on a bad day. They make it a day, two tops before a swarm of lawmen arrive with zero warning. The cabin is surrounded by police, and they are not in the mood for any shit.

Dutch peels back a rag posing as a curtain. Like a switch is flipped, a balls-out gunfight ignites. Shotguns and handguns punch at the shoddy construction.

Bullets fly in every direction. Back and forth like a ballistic shit-fit. Fire begins, spreads to a blaze throughout the cabin. The police hold steady. Dutch and the driver, Lester, fly out the door, fire and smoke pouring out behind them.

The cabin goes up like it was newspaper soaked in gasoline.

The police jump on Lester and Dutch. Dutch looks back at the burning cabin with a knowing sneer. . .

Remo, in mid-stroke. "Most of the crew dies in the fire, including two Mashburn brothers."

Leslie flips a light on, one of those banker's lamps with a green shade.

It illuminates her face as she moves back and forth rhythmically. Around the office is a smattering of quickly removed clothes and empty booze bottles. The 30-something intellectual beauty looks up at Remo, completely shell-shocked. He stares down at her. What?

Remo is older than Leslie by almost ten years, but a damn handsome man with a bar-boy charm that has served him well over the years. It's been stated before that Leslie does this with pricks, and Remo more than qualifies. None of that bothers her right now. It doesn't.

It's not that he's been talking the whole time. Sure, she'd rather the talk be dirty or not at all, but it's not that.

It's not even that she is the Assistant District Attorney assigned to prosecute the very bank crew that Remo has been rambling on about.

What bothers Leslie about all this, what's really throwing a wrench into this potential pleasure fest, is that Remo is one of the top defense attorneys in New York City. Sorry, *the* top defense attorney in New York City, and this bank crew, Mashburn brothers, Lester and the others are. . .

Remo's fucking clients.

CHAPTER TWO

"STOP," snaps Leslie.

Remo explains. "The math on this is simple."

"Can you stop?"

"It's a huge case. I have a bulging box of evidence. You can put them away forever."

"What?"

"What, what?"

"To be clear, you're admitting while we're having sex that your clients are guilty."

"Too weird for you?"

Leslie scrambles off the desk and pulls on some of the balled up clothing on the floor. Her confusion is surpassed only by her hostility.

"You unbelievable shithead."

Drunken state showing, Remo stumbles while trying to find his pants, yanking open the curtains as he falls and hits the hardwood. It's the middle of the day and sun lights up the room. Through the window is a magnificent view of Manhattan.

Leslie wants out of there, fast. She tries to get her head around this situation.

This Remo Situation.

"I am the fucking prosecuting attorney, and you're telling me how to put your clients in jail forever?"

Remo slides over to the cabinet, pouring himself a foot-sized tumbler of Johnnie Walker Blue. He gives her that damn smile.

With her last bit of dignity, she fires, "Fuck you, Remo. My team is going to win this case . . . cleanly."

"Highly doubtful." She'd defend herself, but he's right. Damn it. He takes a large gulp of booze, then pulls a box from under his desk. The box is packed. You can't even close the thing, files and photos almost spilling out. A bursting, spewing, geyser of evidence. Leslie's eyes nearly pop.

"I can't take that."

"It's not that heavy."

"Remo, I cannot accept the box."

"Leslie, your team is fairly shitty."

Complete disbelief that he said it, but she knows he's right.

"You will lose," Remo clarifies. "Look at it this way: you get to help the world be a better place, with orgasms to boot. That's as Kennedy as it gets."

"Orgasms?"

"Seemed like your eyebrow twitched."

"Why are you doing this?"

Remo pops a pill. Ritalin. It's a delicate balancing act with the booze, but Remo has mastered the chemistry. He washes it down with a gulp of Johnnie Blue. Pours a fresh one. He'd rather not give his reasons.

Leslie has heard the rumors. Remo has had a few problems, to put it mildly. Something about a wife who left, and a kid. Somebody said something about that during a lunch, but Leslie can't remember the details. One of those things you hear and give a forced-compassion response like, "Oh, that's horrible," or "Man, that's tough. Is he ok?"

That kinda shit.

Leslie gives a similar response now, thinking she knows what's up. "You're going through a rough patch."

Remo barely appreciates her efforts, gives her his rebuttal. "I'm living a dream."

"Come on, even an emotional dumpster fire like you has to acknowledge it. Everybody knows. The drinking, the pills, the whatever...and now you're throwing cases. Your behavior is suspect, at best."

Remo is a blank slate.

She tries to pry the humanity from him. "Your wife went bye-bye. Have you ever even met your son?"

"That . . . that has nothing to do with this thing . . . here." Now it's all over him, because it has everything to do with this thing here. He redirects. It's what he does for a living, for Christ's sake.

"You have sex with the defense, I win your case for you, and you call me a shithead. Flat-out fucking rude."

She continues getting dressed.

Remo continues drinking.

She says, "Healthy people have a cathartic moment of clarity and give up the pills and sauce."

Remo mulls that idea for a second. "That sounds awful." He pushes the box toward her. "This is a onetime thing."

She thinks, then asks, "The money?"

"Wow. Hookers are less direct than you."

"No, fucker, the money from the bank. The three point two million they stole."

"Oh, I dug that up."

"What?"

Remo shrugs.

"Well fucking hand it over."

"Don't fucking have it."

"Where the fuck did it go?"

"You know that foundation for the families of the bank robbery victims?"

Leslie nods.

"Gave it to them."

"What?"

"The city offers health insurance. Your hearing is horrible."

"Bullshit. Which locker at what train station is it stuffed in?"

"I. Don't. Have. It. Gave it to a good cause. That so hard to believe?"

Leslie's eyes bore through him. Yes, it's extremely hard to believe that a guy like this even knows how to do that. You could hand him a donation bag of used clothes and shoes, drive him to the front door of the local Goodwill, he still couldn't pull it off.

Remo replies, "Take the box. Win the case and you'll get hired to a better gig. Or you can run the risk of being that prosecutor who tried to trade sex for a guilty verdict."

Leslie stares daggers as she struggles with her whirling thoughts. Is he right? Yes. Does she have a choice? Yes, but the right choice, not taking the box, does her no good whatso-fuckingever. Eventually, as per usual, the low road wins. She grabs the box as she heads for the door. "You are a stunning asshole. Thanks for the guilty-in-a-box and the god-awful sex."

Remo stops her, his face now reflecting a surprising, almost alarming amount of sincerity. All the bullshit is gone, the slickness washed away. "Promise me these monsters will never be able to do this again."

Leslie takes in his complete shift in tone, his new body language, and can't help but be moved. This is the man who got her into bed...well, on a desk. This is a man with a heart and perhaps, God forbid, a soul. She understands there is a real reason for what he is doing. She hopes it's a good one, and not that he stole the damn money to flush it away on hookers and blow.

Realistically, she knows that cocaine and boob jobs are exactly where that boatload of blood money is headed, but for the moment, this moment, she'd like to believe Remo is better than that.

The idealistic, hopeful little girl in her can't help but respond, "I promise."

CHAPTER THREE

THE PLAN?

Simple.

Murder multiple motherfuckers, save one asshole.

This is the strategy of one Lester Ellis, a former criminal, former wheelman, current man of the Lord. Lester's résumé, if he ever felt the need to pen one, would read:

"July 1968 to February 2012: Murdering Thief -- Team player. Individual contributor. Fluent. Six Sigma.

"February 2012 to Present: Servant of God -- Six months experience. (But a good six months, you judgmental ass.)"

Lester: weathered, seasoned, bleary-eyed, and beaten down by years of dirty deeds. He stands along an empty road some thirty-odd miles north of New York, surrounded by not a whole helluva lot. Behind him lies the unmistakable outline of a sprawling fifty-five acres on the east bank of the Hudson River known by most as Sing Sing maximum security prison.

His body is a wandering contradiction of personal philosophies. Tats tell the tale of a confused, or at the very least conflicted, man. A Swastika rests on one side of his neck, with a sad clown on the other. A large cross with Jesus nailed to it is scrawled from blade to blade on his back. "FuckU" on one of his shoulders. The cherry on top? On the fatty part of his right paw, etched in crude prison-blue fashion: "Right Hand of God."

He carries few earthly possessions in his thick hands save for his prized cigar, which is barely holding together, a plastic bag that contains a roll of duct tape, and a Bible. The guard working the release counter thought it was kinda strange when Lester asked for the duct tape. Lester proceeded to point to the holes in his boots. What the hell does the guard care? Lester readjusts the crude silver tape job that holds his footwear together.

His fingers rub along his Bible, caressing it. This is not some cheap-ass Motel 6 bible. This thing has some weight, with a hard binding built to stand up to time, and gold accents with touches of tough leather designed to protect the word of the Lord.

Thoughts bounce. Thoughts of the life he's led. Thoughts of the life he's going to lead. Thoughts of how he's going to find salvation for the wicked he has done, if that's even possible. Can you forgive the killing? The stealing? The severing of limbs? The blood Lester has spilled during his lifetime could fill an Olympic-size pool. The money he's made off of it could fill a needle...and it did. Can all the wrongs be washed away by recently letting the Lord in? By performing a righteous act or two? Can that kinda shit be forgiven?

Good Book says it can. Sing Sing preacher man says it can. Gotta give it a shot, what the hell else is he gonna do? Go back to that life? Back to the shit that put him in a hole for the better part of his life, shoved him farther and farther away from the Lord? Not fuckin' likely. To Lester, this is a new day with a new path. One that will deliver him from evil...even if that means inflicting a touch of evil in the process.

Lester closes his eyes tight while he mutters a few holy words under his breath.

Pops his lids open. He's ready now. A horn blares, jolting

Lester from his perfect moment of introspection. His eyes squint, verifying the vehicle kicking up dirt is headed his way.

Yup, that's his ride.

A slightly used black Escalade—a fine mode of criminal transport a few years ago—dented here and there with four unmistakable bullet holes peppered around the hood. The Escalade makes a sudden stop, a drop of the power window revealing the driver—Bobby Balls from Remo's story.

But unlike in Remo's story, he's very much alive.

Bobby Balls smiles wide while greeting Lester. "You ready, sweetheart?"

Lester checks the back, spotting two other criminals. The young one, a punk of a bastard begging to show you how hard he is, answers to Country.

On the other side sits an ice shard of a man with a piercing gaze that makes pit bulls piss. A man who'd gladly cause the suffering of fools way before he'd even consider suffering one himself. One who's spent his years without knowing remorse. Goes by the name of Ferris Mashburn.

Yup, all three of them are very much alive. Sizing up the occupants of the car, Lester makes his way to a passenger-side door. He tosses the cigar, grips the plastic bag in one hand, bible in the other. As he takes in a deep breath of fresh air, he looks to the heavens and mutters a few more silent words before plopping down in the Escalade's passenger side.

Ferris starts in. "We cool?"

Lester gives a nod as he rubs a finger across the bible.

"Fuck yeah we are," from Country. "That fucker is dead as Dillinger."

Nothing but a searing gaze from Ferris, then, "Nobody touches the lawyer until Dutch gets loose." Eyes Country in the back. "Get me?"

"Fuckin' why?" fires Country.

"Because that's how Dutch wants it—"

"Fuckin' retarded."

"—which means that's how we want it. More importantly, that's how a subhuman half-wit like you wants it. Clear enough?"

Lester slowly removes the duct tape from the bag. No one notices.

Country starts in again. "I know big man Dutch wants to be the one to end the motherfucker, but he's locked up, and we're out, and I'm really fuckin' tired of being in hiding. It sucks. We got Chicken Wing on the lawyer right now, watchin,' just waitin' for the green light. We go in, blow that legal eagle to shit, get our money and ride off into the sunset as soon as Dutch joins the party. Pretty fuckin' simple if you ask me—"

Ferris stops him midsentence. The heart-freezing glare, along with Ferris's fingers tightening around his voice box, puts an end to Country's debate. They roll on in silence, the energy in the car having been sucked up and held hostage by Ferris.

"We've been in hiding, that's correct. What's also correct, the point you're missing, is that we've been waiting for the right time, and that time has presented itself. Now."

Country gives a guttural sound, works as a *yes*.

Ferris eyes Lester. "You're a quiet prick."

Lester caresses the Bible. Country continues to gasp and squirm.

"Heard Lester found Jesus or some shit," adds Bobby Balls.

"I did," Lester replies.

Lester watches the countryside, but not for the view. He's looking for something in particular. Setting his bible down next to him, he rests the plastic bag on top, starts to peel a small bit of the duct tape off the roll. Makes a starting pull at the tape as discreetly as can be. No one notices, except Ferris, who's starting to eye the back of Lester's head.

Country is a second or two from passing out. Ferris releases him from his near-death grip. Country slips into a ball in the corner of the backseat. Where he belongs.

Bobby Balls continues, “Tell me, why do you people always find God in the joint? Is it to cling to something, or is it more about hope? Hoping that some magic man in the sky will help you while you’re taking five black cocks in the shower?”

Country cackles with laughter, starting to feel his blood flowing again.

“Something like that, I suppose,” says Lester, still scanning the outside world.

Without looking down, he has taken the plastic bag in one hand and attached the free bit of duct tape from the roll. Has a finger gripped around the roll as if ready to pull, plastic bag at the ready in the other.

“I mean, seriously. When they say find Jesus...the fuck does that even mean?”

Ferris keeps watching Lester. Lester keeps watching the road. Country keeps laughing.

“What is Jesus going to help you do? I mean, now that you found his ass.” Bobby Balls giggles childlike, amused with his own questions.

Lester’s eyes stop. He’s found what he wants through the front window.

“Come on, man, I’m just fucking with you. But really, what are you and Jesus going to do?”

Lester cracks the slightest of grins as he gives his answer. “Murder multiple motherfuckers, save one asshole.”

Everyone except Lester has been slapped with a healthy dose of “what the fuck?” A perfect, silent slice in time. The plastic bag flies over Bobby Balls’ head. In a single move, Lester rolls the duct tape around Bobby's neck two, three times, sealing the bag. The words "Right Hand of God" flex on his hand as Lester works the tape. Leaves the roll attached, bouncing as Bobby Balls fights for air, plastic sucking in and out with a panic-stricken rhythm. It's sick, lacks compassion, but it does give a nice beat you can tap a toe to.

"The fuck?" Country screams, making a dive from the backseat toward the front, 9mm pulled. As he does, Lester grabs the wheel, cutting hard toward a line of trees just off the road.

The Escalade slams head-on into a tree, a jarring collision of bark and steel. Country launches from the backseat—a low IQ javelin—face-first into the windshield. Nose-first, actually, with a crunch of bone and snap of spine, leaving a pulp-faced corpse.

Air bags deploy a fraction of a second after Country's lifeless body bounces from the glass. Ferris's seatbelt snaps him back, as does Lester's. The whole string of events takes only a few seconds. One dead. One working on dying. Two left to kill each other.

The Escalade ricochets off the tree, skidding to a stop. Fluids spit from the hood. Windshield's a spider web, with clumps of Country's face and hair stuck in it. Bobby Balls gives a couple of dying jerks and spasms.

He's hanging in there. God bless him for trying.

Ferris pulls his .357, squeezing off two blasts at Lester. An air bag takes the blast as Lester pops the seat belt free, spinning out the door.

The eerie quiet that comes after a car crash fills the air. All that violent, sudden energy expended in a sliver of time, leaving you with a pile of life-altering devastation. Granted, most car crashes are not the byproduct of a recently released Jesus-freak suffocating the driver with a plastic bag, but it's the same result as a soccer mom blowing through a stop sign while on her cell babbling about shoes—shit you don't want.

Ferris stumbles out, his .357 tracking as he makes his way around the back. Legs wobbly as he tries to get his post-car-wreck bearings, he clears the back bumper and is met by the solid binding of Lester's Bible, which makes a low, muted thwack, connecting with Ferris's face. Leaves his vision spotted with white blobs of light. It only lasts a moment, but that's just enough for Lester to get to his feet and land a crack-punch. Drops Ferris to the dirt. They go at it like wild dogs fighting over the last scrap of meat. Not elegant. Not choreographed. Criminals are beating one another's ass, life and death on the line.

A 4Runner filled with high school kids pulls up. The bearded, hipster driver pokes his head out the window.

"You guys ok?"

Lester pops up, having wrestled away the .357. Ferris bolts, putting a foot on the 4Runner's hood as he springs over. Opening fire, Lester's shots pop holes across the kid's hood, barely missing Ferris as he escapes into the woods.

Kids in the 4Runner give bloodcurdling, scared-shitless wails as they haul ass outta there. Lester lowers the gun, less than satisfied at Ferris giving him the slip. Bobby Balls falls from the car, still hanging in there. God bless him. He's managed to pull the bag off and is crawling away. Lester casually puts two bullets in him.

His mind drifts back to the second bullet point of his plan.

Oh yes, something about saving one asshole.

CHAPTER FOUR

"ASSHOLE?" Mr. Crow barks. "Have you listened to one damn thing I've said?"

Crow, a dapper, well put-together criminal of means, sits across from Remo Cobb, his high-priced defense attorney. Not a hair out of place, suit immaculate. Watch costs more than your car.

Remo gives the tiniest flash of eye contact. "All ears on this side of the table."

Not really; he's preoccupied. He's attempting to bounce a pill into a half full scotch glass that has been carefully positioned between him and Crow. A fun little game of pharmaceutical quarters.

Crow grows more and more annoyed with each bouncing Ritalin. "If the bitch would have just done things right we wouldn't be in this spot."

"Meaning you would have stopped just shy of crushing her windpipe?"

"It got out of hand. She got out of line. I was having . . . a what? A 'day,' let's say. She just ... stopped breathing."

The two men are surrounded by wall-to-wall leather- bound

legal books, polished oak and brass. A private meeting area at the most prestigious New York legal firm that ill-gotten gains can buy. Same office Remo was in with that prosecutor, Leslie. People are still getting fucked, but a much different meeting is in progress.

"I did it. Can't lie. But she pushed me. She pulled a blade for Christ's sake."

"Shit." Remo's response has nothing to do with Crow's story. He missed the damn glass again.

Crow grows more annoyed as a pill flies by his face. "My sight went white. Next I know she's not breathing."

Remo misses. "Cocksucker."

"Am I bothering you?" asks Crow.

Remo glances up. Now he's growing annoyed at his client for interrupting his efforts.

"No?" asks Crow.

Remo is not nearly as well put together as his client. Suit's a mess. Eyes like red pinholes. He was a good-looking man at one time. Now he looks like he's been on a multiyear bender. Crow, previously completely focused on his dead-hooker dilemma, suddenly realizes this asshole attorney, the one he's paying a mint for, is not even vaguely paying attention to his plight. And in Crow's mind, there's a massive bit of plight, goddamnit. "You think you can pay attention, you son of a bitch prick cocksucker?"

Remo bounces a pill, landing one with a plop in his glass of Johnnie Walker. Shoots his arms up in the air as if draining a buzzer-beater at the Sweet 16, then raises a single finger, stopping the now red-faced Crow before he can lay into him with a blitz of heartfelt profanity. He throws back the booze, along with the swimming pill.

It's hard to decipher if Remo has more disdain for his job, life, or Crow. Silence permeates the room. They sit eyeing each other like fighters circling, determining how to dismantle each other. Crow hates that he needs Remo almost as much as Remo hates that he needs Crow. Crow stops himself from blowing up, slips into a smile, deciding to break his lawyer down with a different method. The truth.

"Remo fucking Cobb."

"Present."

"Straight outta Cut and Shoot, Texas."

"Great town. You'd do well there."

"Daddy died in a backroom card game. Mommy? Nobody knows. You're a walking, talking hillbilly lullaby."

"That's the rumor," Remo says after a gulp of scotch.

"Made a name working small cases around Texas. Then you caught the eye of a big swinging dick firm in New York City. Got some motorcycle gang off or some shit, right? Must have been hard shedding that dumbass Texas accent while chewing up d-bag, Ivy League Jews." Crow takes a calculated dramatic pause for fun, then, "Also managed to lose a family along the way."

The family statement sticks at something in Remo, deep. He shakes it off, pushes it down. Swishes a mouthful of Johnnie Blue while eyeballing Crow, absorbing the unrelenting, unnecessarily hurtful truth Crow is telling.

"This path of most resistance made you into the man you are today, and that man? This Remo? Is a USDA certified, Grade-A, grain-fed asshole."

Remo's had enough. "The body gone?"

"The body?"

"The girl. Her body. The shell that carried her soul. Remember? You killed her with your bare hands? Sorry, the one who stopped breathing. I mean, let's table your unfortunate murder habit, and forget the people who might care about these women."

"This isn't my first rodeo," sneers Crow.

Remo pours another drink.

Crow, slightly offended: "You gonna offer me a drink?"

"You shouldn't drink."

"Should you?"

"Absolutely."

"Can you take care of this thing or no?"

"Yeah."

"Yeah?"

Remo shakes his head. It truly yanks at his guts to say but he says it anyways, "I can ease your troubled mind and heal your heavy heart."

"Fuck you, Remo."

"Much appreciated." Remo gulps, then slams the empty glass down.

Every word out of Crow's mouth was accurate. Why the hell does the truth have to come from a wretched human being like that guy? That fucking guy? Remo doesn't go to a therapist. He should, heaven knows he should, but he doesn't. Doesn't see the point, doesn't believe in it, and, damn it, he's not going to. However, his inner thoughts and feelings—some may call them demons—seem to come to the surface while talking to these dregs of society.

Should he just lie on the couch while taking these client meetings?

Remo knows the truth of his life. He's lived the history. Which is precisely why he drinks and pops those pills.

Fucking *duh*. Not a supernatural mystery of the universe. He's no Bigfoot. Unfortunately, substance abuse doesn't make memories or present truths or lifelong demons disappear. It might later on in life, but even if Remo makes it to old age and can't remember the past, who gives a shit? It's today that's rough for him. The here and now is a fucking mess. Besides, if his current behavior can shave those later shitty years off his life, so be it.

Remo knows his life. Doesn't necessarily hate it. Doesn't exactly love it either. It is what it is. That's what people say when they can't, or don't want to, explain a fact of life, right?

All this fuels the synaptic fireworks that are Remo's mental state as he stumbles through the city, in and out of crowds, hours blurring until he finds himself at Gramercy Park. He watches kids playing at a crazy pace, an army of youth without a care in the world. Dogs being chased and giving chase in return. Moms and nannies keep a watchful eye. A safe distance away, a distance where he can't be seen, Remo sits, still dressed in his pricey, mussed up suit which hangs on him like a hanger made of old bones.

He pulls a small pair of binoculars from his coat pocket. He keeps them there, just in case. He begins spying on the children. Actually, he's spying on one child and mother in particular. The three-year-old boy is Sean, his beautiful mother, Anna.

Remo's not a perv. He is a lot of unsavory things, but pervert isn't on the list. Well, not the kind who goes to the park to look at little boys. Jesus, how fucked up is the world when you have to explain that in order to clear the air?

It is what it is. Remo knows Anna and Sean. Cares about Anna and Sean. Anna picks Sean up, spinning him around. Happiness doesn't begin to cover it. Remo watches on for a moment. It's hard to make out his purpose. He sets down the binoculars. Shades of sadness and rising ripples of regret hit him. He wishes he were with them. No time for that shit—that thinking, feeling shit you hear so much about. Remo sparks a one-hitter, looking for some clarity, letting the smoke roll into his lungs and back out.

Flushing out his system. A mother with her newborn bundle of joy pushes an all-terrain jogging stroller near Remo. He's now all but spread-eagle in the grass. She stops, giving him more than a hint of disapproval. *What is wrong with this city?* She moves closer to get his attention, thinking her mere look of disdain will somehow shame this disgusting man into submission.

Remo rolls over, notices her and her look. "Go fuck yourself, lady."

Remo falls into his apartment, flipping on the lights, exposing a magnificent two bedroom in a Murray Hill high-rise. Most would kill half, or all, their family to live here—the best of everything, with a jaw-dropping view of the city. The space is big, filled with many expensive things, yet feels empty, deeply hollow.

The silence is deafening.

He checks the fridge. Nothing but three variations of mustard, some fancy imported beer and a pizza box.

Turns on the TV. Flips around. All dog shit. Checks the fridge again. Hasn't changed. He slips on some headphones, plays some old Violent Femmes. He loves music, even more when he's completely ripshit-hammered.

Uncorks a bottle of wine. Pours a glass. Pops a pill. Drinks.

Tries to sing. Tries to dance. Sucks at both. Catches a glance of his rhythmic ineptitude in the mirror. "Jesus." Grabs his keys, exiting as quickly as he can. Remo's destination is a hipster bar if ever there was one.

Wall Street masters of the universe, young law firm royalty and generic d-bags of all shapes and sizes mingle in the elite watering hole. Men and women trolling for a hook-up. Remo cuts through with drunken grace, with purpose. His target is clear.

At a far end of the room is the quintessential hot bartender. Her name escapes Remo at the moment. Late twenties, Old World gorgeous with New World tits. She works magic, slinging sauce in every direction—a blur of booze and mind-bending sex appeal. Men kneel and worship at her feet.

She knows it. It's what keeps her in business, and business is good. Her focus is unbreakable until she spots her man. Her present love, her way out of an hourly wage.

Her meal ticket.

She stops everything and lights up of the sight of Remo. "Hey, baby."

There's some sexual history here. Everyone sees it. Pisses off the army of hard dicks hoping to be the one she'll pick. She never does—most hot bartenders don't—but it doesn't stop the boys from playing the lottery. Got to be in it to win it, and somebody has to win... right?

She leans over the bar, putting her hands on Remo's face while laying on a sloppy kiss that would strike down mortal men. Breasts saying hello. A twenty-two-year-old bond trader may have passed out. Remo knows they're all watching him. He loves that they're watching. He loves her. Well, not *her*. Loves her chest. Of course he does. It helps to fill the pit a bit. It won't last. Like eating Chinese food or sniffing glue. All good for a while, but it doesn't stay with you long.

They retreat to a converted warehouse loft in Midtown. Nice place, but trying hard not to be too nice. Cool, but trying hard not to be too hip. Expensive, period. On the bed, the hot bartender rides Remo with abandon. Bites her lower lip, squealing like an over-caffeinated porn star.

Remo is bored out of his mind, his dead eyes staring at her and her show.

Glances at the clock, then back to her. Formulates a plan. Remo forces out some bad acting. "That's it. There it is."

"Oh yeah? Do it, Remo. Come for your girl."

He gives it final thrust, adds a twitch to make it look good, along with a somewhat convincing grunt. He lies still, hoping she bought it. She stops bouncing, a little confused and not sure how to handle this.

"Did you come, Sugar Bear?"

"Yup, mind-bending."

"Really? It just didn't seem like you did."

"I have a condom on, so it's not really the bareback kinda fireworks."

"I know, but—" She slides off him. Something is bothering her as she pulls her clothes from the floor. Sure, she likes not having to pay for things. Nice things. She likes having the little things that make life special for her. But dammit, there needs to be a little respect, too. Just a little bit. She deserves that much. Sex with someone you don't like isn't as easy as it looks. She starts to say it, stops, then says it anyway.

"You don't respect anything about me."

Remo sinks. "Ah, fuck."

"No, really. What do you respect about me?"

"There's so many."

"Come on, Remo. One thing. Name one thing."

"I—look, you're a great girl."

"Thank you. And?"

He thinks. It hurts. It hurts to think at all, given the booze, pills and fake orgasms, but it's even harder to come up with a single thing to tell this woman. Whatever her fucking name is. She becomes more and more pissed as the pause drags out. She looks at him as sincerely as a naked, surgically-enhanced woman can.

"Well?"

With no other options, Remo attempts the truth.

"You're a twenty-eight-year-old bartender with a BMW, condo, and tits, who I happily picked up the tab for—what's not to respect?"

Without even a "fuck you," she throws her shirt on in a huff, heading for the door.

Not a great time for the truth. Remo does respect the tits, just not what they're attached to. He tries to make a quick, last-ditch effort to bring them back.

"My place in the Hamptons this weekend?" The door slams behind her. "Sugar Bear?"

That could have gone better. It started out nice. Fuck it.

Remo's hungry.

CHAPTER FIVE

REMO TAKES refuge at an all-night Chinese joint. He's nestled himself into a throne of a booth in the 24/7 dive. Red tablecloths, cheap paper lanterns. A drunk's after-hours haven. His mind drifts as he stares out the large picture window. He lets his head unwind as he watches New York breeze by effortlessly, people moving through the city, through their lives. He looks on glassy-eyed. Lost. Wanting. Like a puppy left in the rain.

He gets caught up in the pace of his wandering mind. There's a lot going on in that head. Still can't shake his conversation with Mr. Crow. The sting of his words hasn't faded. People have said many horrific things to him before— nothing new—but that conversation is doing a number on Remo. His memory slams back to his father. It always does. Daddy Cobb was a hard, hard man. Loved the sauce, hated keeping a job, not much use for Remo. The day Remo's mom went AWOL, Remo remembers asking his dad, "Will she be back?"

"No."

"Where is she?"

"Does it matter?"

"Is she ok?"

No response. Later, when Remo was around ten, he found out she left them; remarried and even had a new baby. Can't blame her. Remo never looked for her. Even with the vast resources currently at his disposal, he's never tried. His firm could find anybody, anywhere, but she wanted out, so she's out.

It is what it is.

Not many people these days have their dad die in a gunfight while cheating a card game. Remo did. In a way, he takes pride in it. Others might say, "My dad died from Alzheimer's at this nice home we found for him," or "He fought the good fight, but cancer ultimately won." Not Remo. "My dad shot two men down after he caught a hanger off the bottom of a stacked deck and, shortly after that, caught two slugs from a .45—one in the chest, one between the eyes."

How would you rather go? Again, it happens. A fifty-something Asian waitress drops off a plate of shrimp fried rice as big as his face, along with a cup of black coffee. At fifty-something, she looks twenty. *These people don't age,* Remo thinks. He addresses the shrimp-laced pile with a fork in hand. Pauses, pushes the plate away. Pulls a silver flask, twists off the top and pours some booze into his coffee, stirs it with his finger.

Remo is forced to hit "pause" on memory lane as some guy tries to get his attention.

The guy does more than that. The guy slides into the booth across from Remo.

Weathered, seasoned, beaten by years of dirty deeds. Body art a wandering contradiction of personal philosophies.

A confused, or at the very least conflicted, man. Lester speaks.

CHAPTER SIX

"REMO COBB." Remo barely glances up from his plate—hurts to focus—and the expression he manages to pull together is one of indifference and intoxication.

Lester sits and rubs his bible while staring at Remo. Watching, taking in everything about him, studying him, working through his feelings about this man and suppressing the ill will. Remo takes note of Lester's appearance, tries to place the face. He can't seem to remember this guy, but feels like he should.

Some burn-out from high school?

That crazy ass-clown from down the dorm hall in college?

Booze typically makes positive recognition challenging, but this one is particularly difficult. Remo attempts, nonetheless, to identify the man sitting across from him, asking, "I know you?"

Lester sits stone-faced for a moment that stretches forever—beyond and back again—then utters, "You do."

Remo's brain gives off a vague spark, ignites a flicker of recognition. "Client?"

"I was."

"All right. What the hell you want?" Remo drifts back to his meal, with its coffee and sauce chaser.

"My name is Lester, and I'm on a mission of mercy."

Remo spots the God tat on his hand, then the Bible. *Jesus freak. Fuck me.*

Lester continues, "I was imprisoned. During that time I learned the grace and glory of a righteous path. A road to redemption, the way the Lord wants me to be. Wants me to save you." Lester is well aware the ears across the booth from him are deaf to his words, but feels he has to at least say these things. Sort of like a disclosure statement for a car ad ("professional on a closed course, do not attempt"), or a cigarette box ("smoke these and die slowly and horribly"). Everybody knows, nobody cares, still, it has to be there.

Remo halts his rice and spiked java intake. "Fan-fucking-tastic."

"Please don't interrupt me, sir."

"Please go away, cocksucker."

Lester feels the rushing wave of anger rip down his spine. He remembers a time when that ripping sensation meant someone was going to be hurting, really bad, really soon. That was a different time, a different Lester. He holds those bad thoughts back now. The thought of jamming that fork into Remo's eye? Currently on the back burner. The idea of dragging Remo from this booth and stomping a boot through his teeth? Held back. That simple notion of wrapping his fist around this lawyer's neck until there's a single snap? Please hold. In lieu of these proven problem-solving techniques, Lester grits his teeth and goes with the coping mechanisms he learned inside. Breathes through his nose. Finds his calming voice, his happy place. Exhales the hate and says, "I'm asking you politely to listen to what I have to say. I've come a long way for you."

Remo, who considers holding back and exhaling hate techniques for pussies and homos, opts for another method. He covers his face with his hands. From behind his fingers, he replies,

"When I move my hands, I'd like you to be gone." He gives it a beat and then removes his hands.

Lester's still there.

Frustrated, annoyed and flat-out fucking done with God Boy, Remo barks out, "Pretty please, fucking dissipate."

Lester slams his Bible to the table. Hard. The kind of slam that makes one think, *I shouldn't have said that.* Shrimp and coffee jump as Lester's cold, hard eyes burn with an unmistakable intensity. The room drops to a low murmur. Other tables look on while trying hard not to seem like they are. The uncomfortable seconds crawl. The air feels tight; at least it does to Remo.

Lester lets the entire restaurant off the hook by finally speaking. "You have wronged people in your life, correct?"

Nothing from Remo. He's pretty sure Lester knows the answer without him saying it.

Lester asks harder this time. "Correct?"

Remo gives in. "One or two."

"Yes. Yes, you have." Lester grabs a giant scoop of shrimp fried rice with his bare hand, inhaling it. Remo is trying hard not to be disgusted by this poor man's Tebow shoving his paw into his food.

He asks, "You mentioned saving me?"

Lester gives a nod.

"From..."

"Men are coming to kill you." Lester wipes the excess rice from his mouth.

Remo watches a carrot cube land on the table, then asks, "One more time?"

"You recall a devil named Dutch? Evil brothers named Mashburn? Ferris? Chicken Wing?"

Remo's life hits pause. Face drops. Heart freezes. Every molecule of his being slams on the brakes, flips and catches fire. Oh hell yeah, he recalls. Throwing the case. Digging up the money. Fuck. Fuck. Fuck. Total recall sets in, Remo now remembering how he knows this man. "You drove getaway."

"Yes." Lester flicks the carrots cube away.

"How the hell are you out?"

"An organization named Prisoners for Faith got me a new attorney and found some holes in the case against me."

Remo's blood pressure spikes. How could Leslie fuck that up?

Lester takes Remo's shaking hand. "I'm a man of the Lord. I've been given a second chance and I cannot, will not, allow them to hurt you. I'm here to save you."

Remo pulls away. This is entirely too much for him to process in the moment. Hard to process in a lifetime. Too much for anybody to process, but for Remo, in his condition, this is just too damn much.

Lester prompts, "You threw our case."

Remo knows the truth will not set him free in any way, shape or form. He attempts to cover the obvious truth, but Lester cuts him off. Saving Remo from throwing one more lie on the fire. "You lost on purpose. You lost the case against Dutch and me. It's all right, Remo. No hate from me. I'm a better man for it."

"I didn't throw your case. I got beat. Big difference."

"You stole their money."

"What? What money? I did nothing of the sort."

Lester's dagger-stare puts an end to Remo's bullshit.

Remo recoils, leaks out, "Okay. Fine. Got me. I threw the case, but I don't have the money. I gave it to a good cause."

"Of course you did."

"I did, damn it."

Lester smiles as he snatches another handful of rice, thinking how damn good it is. He thinks about ordering some more. Perhaps an egg roll. Pork, not that vegetarian shit. He's for God and all, but the man enjoys meat. Maybe some of that fried pork with the red shit on top.

Remo's mind couldn't be any farther away. He's thinking of red shit all right, he's thinking about his blood seeping out from multiple bullet wounds. Hell, that's if he's lucky. These Mashburn boys like to get creative when disposing of people they dislike. With Remo sitting at #1 atop on the Mashburns' most wanted list —yeah, they'll work up something really super special for their best buddy Remo. His defense mechanisms kick in, and he thinks *this can't be happening.* Thinks *it is simply not possible.*

Thinking out loud, Remo utters, "Dutch is in jail. His brothers and the rest of their crew are corn-holing Hitler in hell."

"They didn't die in that fire," says Lester, trying to flag down a waitress. "Some are dead now of course, by my hand. But the Mashburn brothers? Oh, they've been waiting for the right time to present itself, and they are very alive and very upset with you."

Remo swallows a bit of vomit. Terror-shakes set in, rattling their way down to his toes. He says, "You're out of your skull. Nobody's coming."

Lester looks to Remo with surprisingly kind eyes. "People will come, dear Remo. Nasty, filthy, scary people. People with bad childhoods and questionable morals will descend upon you with guns, bloodlust, and visions of murderous mayhem dancing in their heads. Make no mistake. They are coming."

Remo sits back, letting this life-altering news wash over him, through him. This kind of news is on par with "you've got cancer" or "your liver will explode in 3 to 6 months" or "your balls are going to fall off." He rubs his face, then takes a hard swig from his flask. Skips the coffee. Lester gets frustrated with the waitress, who is clearly ignoring him, and motions to Remo about his plate of unattended fried rice. May I?

Remo pushes it towards him. *Oh please, help yourself.* An ever so delicate sound stops Remo.

Tink, tink, tink.

It's coming from outside the restaurant.

Tink, tink.

Remo looks to the window. A man in a hoodie, dark glasses, and what looks like a very fake beard is tapping on the window with car keys, trying to get Remo's attention. Remo gives the man a *what the fuck now?* look. Lester notices nothing, oblivious, with his face buried in the blissful freedom of Chinese food.

The Hoodie Man points down toward the ground. Remo doesn't get it. The man pulls a nickel plated .357 with a rubber grip. Remo gets it.

Drops down, sliding under the table lightning fast. Hoodie Man opens fire on Lester without a hint of mercy. A relentless pounding of lead blows out the window, glass exploding in a scattershot of bouncing shards which blanket the table and surrounding area. Bullets rip the air, tagging Lester in multiple points of entry, spinning and whirling him out of the booth. Pulpy pops sprout from his body like springtime flowers.

Restaurant patrons scatter like roaches when the lights turn on, screaming and running for the exits. Tables fly, chairs skid across the cheap floor, plates break—this is what happens when bullets come for dinner.

Remo hits the floor under the table, the falling rain of glass dancing around him, contorting into a fetal position in a feeble attempt to gain some form of comfort.

Comfort is now a distant, distant memory for Remo.

One final, bone-rattling blast sends Lester to the floor. The mysterious, gun-toting hostile Hoodie Man bolts into the night, escaping into the cover of darkness.

Lester's body falls, flopping face-to-face with Remo on the floor. Remo tries to find his breath while looking into a dying man's eyes. Blood begins to slowly roll into pools of deep crimson, engulfing the cheap black and white checkered tile. Fear has rendered his legs numb. Breathing is past the point of controlling. Remo fights to stay calm, or as calm as a man can be when his heart is seconds from jumping out through his throat.

As calm as a man can be staring eye-to-eye at his future.

This is the day his life will surely change.

WHAT THE HELL IS WRONG WITH ME?

PART II

CHAPTER SEVEN

AN HOUR later and Remo's face is still plastered in the controlled mental meltdown expression he had on the floor face-to-face with Lester. His mind is a spiraling whirlpool of *what the fuck?* Realizes he could still be having sex with a gorgeous bartender rather than this.

This!

What the hell is wrong with me? What's going to happen to me? Fuck me. The place is now swarming with police, surveying the area, picking through debris for evidence, working the scene. Not much around to pick or work though. Only things there are a blown out window, a shot to hell Chinese joint and a tatted up ex-con clinging to the rim of life. Lester is carted off by EMS. Words and phrases like, "Not gonna make it," "Not looking good," and "Fucked" are thrown around casually.

Remo sits at a table sipping coffee. Across from him is Detective Harris. There's a certain amount of uneasiness between them, people with an unfriendly past. A ton of hate bubbles within Harris, just beneath the surface. He keeps it there in order to maintain a certain level of professionalism, but it's very hard to do. He's held back from beating rapists, murders, and others into unrecognizable puddles, but—like a lot of people—Harris can taste the burning fantasy of beating the piss out of Remo.

Harris is exactly what you'd expect. Big. Fat. Bald.

Asshole.

Harris says, "In your line of work, your sense of right and wrong must be like a pretzel. Meet a lot of hefty bags of shit, don't ya?"

"Clients," replies Remo. Speaking is difficult for many reasons at this moment. The fact he really doesn't want to talk to Harris doesn't help.

"This guy Lester, he one of your shit bags?" asks Harris.

No comment from Remo.

"He say anything of note?"

"Yeah, 'of note'."

"Ya know, off the record... I don't like you. At all."

"Painfully aware."

"Last April you toasted me pretty good on the stand."

Three uniformed cops, along with a few detectives, now stand around. They all stare at Remo like he fucked their sisters then didn't call. Not lost on Remo, he recalls April clearly. Really he just wants Harris to shut the hell up. Perhaps that guy in the hoodie can come back and shoot Harris—or Remo. At this point it doesn't matter to him. Harris keeps riding his train of thought.

"And that disease of a human you set free? The one who killed four more people less than a day later? You recall that little moment, fuckface?"

Remo redirects. "Can we talk about tonight?"

"Sorry, excuse me. On the record again."

"He said people are coming to kill me." A long, silent beat to go with the long, blank stares from Harris and his fellow officers. "You catch that, Detective?"

"Oh, yeah, I got it."

"Thoughts?"

Harris delivers his explanation like he was reading the daily lunch specials. "It's New York. People say shit all the time. I had a homeless guy tell me today that lesbian mutants were planning a global rebellion."

Cute, Remo thinks, but he can't help but consider this may be more of a real threat than the good Detective's dismissive evaluation.

"You said this man at the window instructed you to get down?"

Remo nods.

"Like he was telling you to get out of the way? As if he was only after Lester?"

Remo knows where this is going. "Maybe, but—"

"Doesn't sound like you were the target of any violence here. More like Lester was the one in trouble."

Nothing from Remo. Why argue with a man who doesn't care, hates you, and worst of all... is making sense?

Harris, an annoying gleam in his eye, offers to help. "If, of course, you feel uncomfortable or threatened in any way, I can have some of my best men keep a watchful eye over you."

Remo looks to the gallery of armed lawmen who despise everything about him.

Harris leans in. "Off the record, they hate you too."

No shit.

Outside the eatery, the sun is starting to rise. Through the blown-out window, people are watching real-life crime TV. They can't help but watch as Remo has his little love chat with Detective Harris. Across the street, a small crowd has gathered to gawk and rubberneck at the crime scene. Early morning fun for those coming off the graveyard shift, and even better for those still drunk from last call.

Nestled among the crowd of onlookers is the man in the

hoodie. The man with the .357 who shot Lester all to hell. He's lost the glasses, the hoodie, and the beard, now looks like his true self: a frail, coked-up, weasel of a man who wears a crooked smile and has crazy eyes.

Eyes that are locked on Remo like he was dinner.

This would be Chicken Wing.

CHAPTER EIGHT

CHICKEN WING. A.K.A. the youngest Mashburn brother. At the tender age of 23, Chicken Wing is clearly the most dangerous of a dangerous bunch. He carries a seemingly endless surplus of nervous energy, fueled with a mix of angst and narcotic-enriched psychosis. By any normal standard, an unemployable disaster of a human who operates without remorse, reason or the vaguest sense of right and wrong. Of course the Mashburn family business has a much different set of standards.

The 'Chicken Wing' handle was lovingly given to him by his brothers. When he was a kid, his scrawny frame produced arms that resembled—you got it—chicken wings. He can't remember which one saddled him with the name, but it stuck. Nicknames, a lot like herpes, don't leave you. Ever. He's older now, but still a skinny guy, and his muscle mass hasn't grown enough for his brothers to change the name. Only Chicken Wing's anger and violent tendencies have grown.

His cell rings. He knows who it is without looking. Chicken Wing steps away into a nearby alley. "Yo." A familiar voice crackles on the other side of the call.

A family voice. "You on him?" asks Ferris.

Just as Lester had said, Ferris is alive and well and standing in the middle of a suburban home that looks like it was ripped out of a Pottery Barn catalog. Every knickknack has a story. He plays with a wooden rooster as he talks to his fucked-up brother on a prepaid cell. He smiles, thinking how Chicken Wing would giggle hysterically about Ferris playing with a cock.

"On him? Surely am. Haven't seen any money—"

"He's not going to walk around with three million and change. Probably has it in several safe spots around town." Ferris walks into a warmly decorated living room. He's lived through problems with Chicken Wing, problems that arose from his little brother failing to follow the simplest of orders. Not because the kid is stupid, but because he's an impulsive little nut bag. Ferris knows he has to be very clear with his little brother. "Hear this now. You stay on him. Lester lost his shit today. He took out half the crew."

Chicken Wing grows a big, knowing grin. "Just saw Lester. Put a bucket of bullets in him."

"When?" Ferris closes his eyes, freezing off this new info – *What the fuck did he do? What the FUCK did he do?*

"Just now. He was talking to Remo and—"

"Remo? What did he say to him?" Ferris is about to jump out of his skin, mind flipping through worst-case scenarios. Chicken Wing scenarios.

"How the fuck should I know?" Chicken replies, beginning to simmer toward a boil because of his big brother's big-brother tone.

"Chicken Wing, we talked about control. Remember our talk? Do not—"

"Yeah, I know, Ferris. I saw Lester having dinner with Remo. Didn't look like a good thing, so I took care of it."

Ferris recognizes the defensive spike in his brother's tone, registers it, and pulls it back a level or two, trying to soothe the conversational tone. "And you were right . . . this time. But we can't go reckless with something like this."

His efforts are not working. At all. Chicken Wing's agitation multiplies with every word. "I heard you, for fuck's sake. You always fucking... you worry about your own goddamn chores." Chicken Wing considers throwing the burner phone against the brick wall, but hangs up instead.

Congratulates himself for his maturity.

Ferris pockets his phone, walks into the living room, and takes a seat on the couch. Clearly, he's not happy with his little brother. He can't help but blame himself a bit for putting Chicken Wing in a position of potential failure. Then again, the kid has to grow up sometime. Can't keep mothering the motherfucker. Mutters to himself something about that dumbass little shit fucking up everything.

His self-contained conversation is interrupted by a muffled yelp from the corner of the room. Ferris turns, puts a finger to his lips and waves a cold no-no finger toward a woman balled up on the floor.

A bound, gagged and terrified woman.

When she hand-picked all these knickknacks for her dream house, she never thought life would end up like this. While she carefully scoured countless thrift stores, pored over catalogs and searched online, she never thought she was decorating her own tomb.

Her lips quiver, fighting to obey her home invader's—she didn't catch his name—request for quiet.

Ferris turns on the TV, putting his feet up as he opens a bag of Baked Lays. Baked Lays? Just buy the fucking real ones. Unbelievable. He turns up the volume, ignoring the cries from the woman in the corner.

A picture of a glowing couple rests on a corner table, the woman on the floor during a much happier time. In the picture, she's wrapped in her husband's arms. Her eyes lock on the picture. She thinks that if only her broad-shouldered, strong, courageous husband were here none of this would be happening.

Frank would kill this fucking asshole. This fucking asshole who's eating their Baked Lays and putting his feet up on their brand new Hyde turned-leg coffee table... oh, this fucking asshole.

What she doesn't know, couldn't possibly know, is that her husband is actually painfully aware of what's going on. He's not happy about it, but he knows nonetheless.

He knows because her husband, her Frank, is the same Frank as—

CHAPTER NINE

THE BROAD-SHOULDERED, strong, courageous prison guard stands monitoring the island yard.

Rikers Island to be exact.

Unlike in the happy picture with his wife, Frank's face is wrapped in worry. Smile gone. Beyond tense. The thought of Ferris Mashburn spending some quality time in his home, with his wife . . .

He scans the yard filled with convicts of all makes and models. It's a criminal soup of races, tats and mental twist-ties. Frank zeroes in on one inmate in particular, walking a hard line toward Dutch Mashburn.

Dutch stands alone, watching an inmate basketball game. Whites against blacks. Sure, it's all about race, and does nothing to soothe ethnic tensions, but it does make keeping track of who's on whose team very easy.

Dutch, older than Ferris and considerably older than Chicken Wing, is the undisputed ruler of the Mashburns, the crew and, now, Frank and his wife.

In short, Dutch = Scary Dude.

He was born with the glow of filthy, nasty intelligence, and has the look of a man who would gut your family and then post it as an anatomy lecture on YouTube.

Frank moves closer to Dutch, trying to have an inconspicuous conversation while they watch the nearby game. Struggles to find a tough, strong tone as he speaks. “The bus is set. They’re moving some of the more violent inmates to another facility.”

A tough and strong tone means little to nothing when talking to Dutch. All he gives in return is his standard, ghastly disposition.

Frank continues, “I got myself scheduled to work the bus. That means you need to find a way on it.” He pulls out a crude, prison-made knife, or shiv to those in the suburbs, slipping it discreetly to Dutch.

“Only inmates get hurt. No guards, right?” asks Frank.

Dutch still offers nothing. Frank hates having to act like customer service to this bastard. He knows the situation, sure, but he has his limits, and he’s just about pushed to the edge. He looks at Dutch, raises his voice to a harder tone. “Listen, you piece of shit. If that monster of yours hurts my wife in any way...”

Dutch's face doesn't even attempt to alter expression.

His heartbeat rests comfortably, as if he were lying on a raft drifting in a pool in Vegas. Dutch was threatened, beaten, shot and stabbed—all before he could drive a car. Not too long after that, Dutch was the one delivering the threats and beat downs. He's shot more people than the LA and Detroit PDs combined. Butchered more poor bastards than Jason Voorhees. Not a whole helluva lot shakes Dutch's tree. Certainly not some prison yard bull who Dutch has by the balls. Which is why Dutch doesn't even give the courtesy of eye contact as he simply replies, "What?"

Frank's blood boils, working him into a lather as he attempts to retort.

Dutch cuts him off. "Was that your big plan? Raising your voice?"

Frank stands down.

"We have a deal, sweet-ass. You do what you want to do and we won't." They lock eyes. Frank has no choice but to trust him. The whole time, Dutch never loses concentration on the basketball court.

"Now, please. I need to go get violent for a moment," says Dutch, whistling as he strolls toward the court. He cuts through the game without pause, forcing the players to alter their movements. He strolls to the center of the court, the mean, high-intensity game in full swing.

Dutch couldn't care less.

He parts the players like the Red Sea, bringing the game to screeching halt. The players surround him. Black and white alike, they've found a common enemy. A mountain of muscle steps up, itching to throw down a ton of unpleasantness. Any reason to unleash pain on someone is an excellent reason. He towers over Dutch.

Mountain snarls, "The fuck, Dutch?" The players crowding around are dying to tear this old guy apart.

Other guards start to take notice.

Dutch, calm as a Hindu cow, gives a disarming crack of a smile before ripping the shiv across the Mountain's neck. So fast, so clean it doesn't even bleed at first. It starts to spit slowly, then gushes like water from a burst dam. The Mountain grabs his neck, blood rushing through his thick fingers.

Shock and disbelief are stuck in his eyes as his life spills out onto the court.

Dutch spins, a devil's holiday, jamming the crude weapon into anyone unfortunate enough to be around him. Inmates fall back, bleed, drop.

Cutting. Plunging. Ripping. Multiple stab wounds for each.

Sounds of thick flaps puncturing skin followed by the stomach-turning tearing from the blade's exit. Dutch moves like a man possessed, lightning fast, an impressive, beautiful blur of violence.

He releases an inhuman, hollow wail. His face expressionless. An atypical outburst for a man like Dutch. He usually conserves his vocal cords, only using them as necessary, but in this situation, he feels it's just the right finishing touch.

The right amount of violent crazy to get him on that bus.

Frank gives it a standing eight count before rushing over to join the other guards as they swarm the scene. They push their way through the crowd, stepping over, and sometimes on, wounded and dying inmates. The group pins Dutch to the court with hands and knees, fat sausage fingers.

Dutch's eyes flare, the pleasure he's drinking in, the excitement, permeates his very bones. Veins pop on his forehead, an insane smile spreads. The ecstasy of the moment, this is what Dutch lives for.

Violence. Death with a purpose. His purpose.

Dutch doing what Dutch does best.

CHAPTER TEN

THE MORNING SUN illuminates the stainless steel fixtures, polished hardwood floors, and high-end upgrades in Remo's apartment. Showroom-quality living, fit for a king.

Remo staggers through the front door looking like he's been hit by a truck then dragged for miles. The events of the previous day have taken their toll. His keys get tossed in one direction, and his shoes fly in another as he storms through the living room en route to the bar.

He pulls his tie free, dumping it into a silk lump on the hardwood. Gulps some Johnnie—sweet, sweet nectar make the bad man go away—while trying to pull himself. Thinks, *Who lives like this? I gotta get my life in order. This is no way for a man to live. Need to start exercising, eating better, be kinder to animals . . . perhaps people.*

Fuck people. Grabs a banana, pours a fresh scotch. It's a start. An envelope slips under the door.

Remo stops cold. His cheeks balloon, filled with Johnnie like a drunk chipmunk.

Remo eyes it, his heart revving, pushing the needle deep into the red. Sets down his scotch and gingerly moves toward the door.

Pokes his head out into the hallway, then allows the rest of his body to follow.

Empty. Nothing. Nobody.

Remo slips back inside, locks the door. He slowly picks up the envelope, treating it like it was a special delivery of anthrax. Takes a long moment, as if not opening it will end whatever the fuck is going on. As if denial will call off the dogs.

The Mashburn family. If only. He slides his finger along the flap, creating a slow tear, opening it ever so carefully. In the back of his head, he thinks of the Road Runner's creativity while trying to elude Wile E. Coyote. With one eye shut, he rips the rest of the envelope open. No anthrax or bomb, but he does find a crudely written note. It reads like an inbred five-year-old— or a profane Santa— crafted it.

We no when U R sleeping. We no when U R awake. Sleep tight, cunt.

Remo's balls might have climbed into his sinuses. His hand shakes as he guzzles more Johnnie. It should burn as it slips down his gullet. Remo's senses are so dull he doesn't even notice. He races to the bedroom. Clothes scatter in every direction as Remo digs through his dresser.

"Come on. Fuck, fuck, fuck. Ah, there you are," he says, finding the Glock 9mm he has tucked away, just in case.

Hello, lover.

He inspects the Glock like he knows what he's doing. Pulls at it, picks at it. "Shit." The clip falls out, dropping to the floor. The Glock was a gift from a client to show appreciation for a job well done. When Remo opened it years ago, his first thought was, *how many times has this been used?* What a nice, tidy way to get rid of a murder weapon—give it to your attorney.

Unbelievable dickhead clients.

Now, however, Remo thinks it's the most thoughtful fucking gift he's ever received. He just wishes he'd gone to the range or taken some damn lessons or something. He jams the clip back in and yanks back the slide like they do on TV.

Blam!

The blast blows out his bedroom window, a deafening sound reverberating through the apartment. Remo makes a mental note to come up with a good lie before calling maintenance with this one. He slips the gun back into the dresser drawer, covering it with underwear. Perhaps going to the gun was a bit premature. He's pretty sure the neighbors are out of town. He'll lie later if he has to.

Remo heads back into the living room, yanks the sprawling picture window's curtains shut.

Throws the remaining three locks on the door. Slides the chain on. Checks the peephole. Jams a chair under the knob.

He doesn't know what else to do. He's defended people who have caused situations like this one. He's even torn apart on the stand the people who were their victims. But he's never been the target. He's not a fan.

Remo digs through the hall closet, finds a baseball bat and backpedals out. *Okay,* he thinks, *you're okay.* On second thought... he switches off the lights.

"Shit," he yelps as he bumps into something, falling to the floor of the now pitch-black apartment.

Fumbling in the darkness, he manages to get a candle lit and sits at the dining room table. Smells like jasmine. Would be a romantic setting, if things weren't so damn shitty.

He takes out his cell and scrolls through the contacts. He stops on one, looking long and hard at the name. Anna. His thumb inches toward "select."

Stops himself. Not the time. Not sure if there *is* a good time. He scrolls on and goes with another number. New York City ADAs are somewhat used to receiving phone calls at all hours, but the rude awakening still pisses Leslie off.

She manages a groggy, "Hello?"

"You fucking suck," Remo announces before hanging up.

Downs the Johnnie and pours a fresh one by dancing candlelight. A self-satisfied smirk spreads across his lips. He can't help but think, *Even in the face of death, I've still got it*.

CHAPTER ELEVEN

THEY SAY when you drink to the point of passing out you don't ever truly achieve a deep sleep. Something to do with the fact that your body is fighting off the alcohol and is unable to relax enough for your mind to completely let itself go. That or maybe your body has some sort of mechanism just underneath the surface that's acutely aware your drunken ass could puke at any moment. Believe it or not, your body doesn't really want you to die choking on your own vomit while passed out. Self-preservation doesn't take nights or weekends off.

Of course, you can override this mechanism by sucking down so much sauce it short circuits nature's little self- preservation helper—see former AC/DC frontman Bon Scott for details. Death by misadventure does not look pretty.

Your brain will allow you to dream while in this alcohol-induced limbo. Perhaps not as peaceful as normal sleep would be, not as fluid. More of a herky-jerky kind of sleep that starts and stops, hits pause, rewinds, then records over the good parts. Over and over and over again, until you wake up feeling like you crawled out of a goat's anus.

Remo prefers this to lucid dreaming.

It's not the sole reason he drinks the way he does, but it's a side effect he welcomes. Real dreams can unlock the head or unconsciously unwind things that are better left in a twisted hairball in the corner.

His dreams tend to be more superficial mental exercises. Comfort food dreams. Something for his brain to chew on while Remo falls under the spell of Ritalin and Johnnie Walker Blue. R&B, he calls it. He saw something somewhere, maybe *60 Minutes,* where college dickheads were taking Ritalin to increase brainpower, allowing them to study/cheat in school. The drug was designed for hyperactive children, but apparently when adults take it the results are slightly different. Instead of mellowing out hyper Jenny or Jack, it allows adults to focus—like really fucking focus—and absorb information at a much greater rate. Of course, there's also talk about it elevating blood pressure, causing strokes and the like, but hell, McDonald's can do that too. Not to mention, Mickey D's does nothing for your grade point average and can make you fat as fuck, so what's a boy to do?

Remo likes the Johnnie Blue, but he's a high-priced, high-profile attorney who needs to be able to focus, be sharp, and retain large amounts of information. The sauce can cause more than a few hiccups with those needs, so it makes perfect sense to welcome the pills to the party.

Mr. Blue does what he does, little boy Ritalin does what he does, and Remo comes out smelling like a rose.

Of course, it hasn't been perfect. Working out a system takes time, and there were moments, especially in the beginning, when he struggled to get the timing, dosage and mix just right. Painful, socially uncomfortable moments. But after a relatively short amount of time Remo got it down and, depending on your personal moral code, he's been pretty successful.

Alcoholics sometimes refer to their time being drunk as "being on the island." Remo thinks those AA cocksuckers probably invented it.

Quitters.

Not that "being on the island" is a bad description. It just sounds so, so...

Fuck it. Remo just doesn't like it, that's all.

Now, during Remo's time on the island, his thoughts tend to bounce and skip from memory to memory, with the occasional blip of fantasy.

Tits and pussy, booze and pills, big-ticket luxuries. More tits. More pussy. Remo surrounded by tits and pussy while in a massive hotel suite, getting a blowjob in a limo, sex with a woman while skydiving, her form flipping between different nationalities and ethnic origins like that chick from the X-Men. Fairly certain there's a blue girl in there somewhere.

Then, surprisingly, his mind goes black.

The kaleidoscope of pornographic images is wiped from his mind, replaced by total, swallowing darkness.

In his dream a door opens. It leads into a dimly lit room. A room lit by the soft glow of a child's nightlight. In the room, a young boy is sound asleep, wrapped up in bed with the covers pulled up to his chin. Remo slumps in a leather office chair nestled in the corner of the room. He wears his best suit and holds a bottle of Johnnie Blue in his hand. He watches the boy but is unable to see his face. The boy's back is turned to him as he lies facing the opposite wall.

A baby cries in the background, somewhere Remo can't see. The sound is piercing. Through the door storms a pack of men armed with shotguns and assault rifles. Their faces are blank, like a pillowcase of skin has been stretched over their skulls.

They stop to look to Remo, then turn their attention to the boy in the bed.

The baby screams louder. Remo looks on emotionless, takes a swig. The men pump their shotguns, lock and load their assault rifles. The baby's screams stop, leaving an eerie silence in the air. The young boy pops straight up in bed as if it was on fire.

His face is pillowcase blank as well, but Remo can still make out his mouth beneath the strained skin. The boy reaches out for Remo and screams in terror.

Remo tries to jump from his chair but falls hard to his knees, fingers fumbling mere inches from the faceless boy.

Shotguns explode. Assault rifles rattle endlessly.

This is not REM sleep.

This is REMO sleep.

CHAPTER TWELVE

REMO JOLTS AWAKE. Not completely awake. It hurts to get there. He cracks his lids open, finding himself still at his dining room table. The candle has burned down to a purple cow turd. He sits upright in the stiff dining chair. All seems well, save for the fact his Johnnie bottle is completely empty.

His head feels like it's on fire, and he realizes he still holds the bat, clutched tightly to his chest. Remo jolts back in the chair when his cell starts ringing, tipping over and landing less than gracefully on the floor. He springs up, bat in hand, fighting to gain some semblance of control. Answers the call.

"You thinking about making it in today, snowflake?" asks the gravel-grinding voice of his boss, Victor.

Remo squeezes his eyes shut, "Rough evening. Cover for me?"

"Fuck you, cover for you. We're buried here."

"Things . . . things are bad," grunts Remo.

"Fascinating. Get in here or I'm sending people to come get you."

Victor's words spark an idea. Remo hangs up, bolting for the door.

Remo looks a mess as he pushes his way through the crowded streets. He constantly checks over his shoulder, working sideways glances to scan faces as they pass by him. His heart pounds at the thought that someone could gun him down at any moment. Can't help but think again, this is no way to live. Thinks about Harrison Ford in *The Fugitive.* That makes his situation seem sexy-cool for about five seconds, then it's back to the sickening tumbling in his gut, a feeling that's starting to become his normal state of being. It's odd, but this feeling is starting to become almost comforting.

Everyone else seems to glide along without a care in the world. Just fluttering about their normal day like all is fine and dandy. Have they no idea about the pain and struggle of others? Actually, Remo realizes he's never given a second thought to any of these things either. Decides to let it go.

Someone bumps into Remo and he jumps back, raising a fist.

"What the fuck?" barks a kind-looking little old lady.

Nice. Even the elderly are giving him shit. Remo tries to get a hold of himself as she passes, muttering something about him being a fucking cocksucker. Lovely woman. Remo cuts through the crowd and enters a building, heading for the floor of his law office. Office of the Gods. He barely makes eye contact with his co-workers. A few try to engage in a "good morning" or two. He stops just short of telling them to fuck off, actually. Remo hates morning chit-chat on a good day, and he sure as hell isn't interested today. Singular focus as he moves to a corner office.

He reaches his corner fortress of solitude, shutting the door behind him. Fires up his laptop while pulling multiple files from a cabinet. In the files he fumbles through photos of now familiar guys. Candid photos, multiple mug shots, and other random photos of Dutch, Lester, the Mashburns and other assorted assholes doing unsavory activities. There's a shot of masked gunmen taking down a bank, followed by a great team photo of the crew—you could put it on a Christmas card. Next ones he pulls are stills of a shot-to-hell bank lobby taken from the surveillance cams.

Pools of blood.

Tape outlines of bodies.

Some, very small bodies.

He turns to his laptop, scanning seemingly endless legal PDFs and .doc files, before finding a video file. Remo leans back. He knows this is the one he was looking for. The one that frightens him. Remo hesitates before clicking it open, knowing what's on it. Wishing he'd never seen it. But he has to see it again. He clicks.

A surveillance video of the bank lobby opens on the screen.

Calm at first, filled with people doing their business. Remo's eyes zero in on a young mother holding a newborn child. He'd warn her if he could. *Run! Get the hell out of there, lady.* It's too late, of course. Hell busts loose as five men in ski masks storm in, armed to the teeth.

The Mashburn crew, crashing the party.

Remo's eyes never leave the mother and child. He knows what's coming. Hates what's coming. Hates what he's seen. Not just here, but what he's seen and defended over the years. He feels sick again, and this time not because of the people coming to kill him. This time he feels sick because he defends these people. He's been paid well for defending these people.

Who does that? He does that. His thoughts are ripped back to the screen by the mix of screams and thundering gunfire. He closes his eyes and covers his ears, trying to force away the horrible sights and sounds of senseless violence. There are a lot of bad things on that video. Bad things that can't be unseen.

Remo pops a pill. Slams the laptop closed. Pulls his iPhone, flips to a picture of a three-year-old boy. Sean from the park. Remo storms into Victor's office, one which leaves no question this is where the boss does his thing. Pleasant work environment doesn't even begin to cover it. Victor, a silver fox of a defense titan, sits, working someone over hard on the phone.

He massages the words like a tiger playing with a ball of yarn.

"Maybe he burned down the building, maybe he didn't. Arson is a strong word to use so casually . . ."

Remo grabs the phone and hangs up.

You'd think Victor'd be pissed, but he's not. An effective leader, Victor knows you have to treat individuals differently. If you produce for Victor, you get the spoils. If you don't, you get a sideways foot up your ass. Remo gets the spoils, and the benefit of doubt that goes along with it.

“Well, fucking hell. You look like you crawled out of a goat’s ass.”

Remo shuts the door, starts closing the blinds.

"What the hell are you doing?"

Remo paces. "I need help."

"No shit."

"People are trying to kill me."

"Who?"

"Bank crew, about a year ago."

Victor scratches his head. "Need more."

"Mashburn brothers."

Zero recognition from Victor.

Remo explains. "Oldest one, Dutch, touch of a violent streak. Middle fucker, Ferris, cool as a cucumber but mean as a snake. Then there’s the little whackadoo they call Chicken Wing.”

"Oh, yeah. Right, right."

"Their getaway driver, dude named Lester, came to me last night."

"You lost that case." Victor likes Remo, but you have to remind even your best employees every once in awhile about their failures. He remembers reading that in some book once during a long flight.

"Big loss. You should have won, if memory serves." Victor gets up.

Remo follows him out the door and they continue their chat while moving through the busy floor. Remo can't help but be annoyed by the conversation—I mean, shit. *People are coming to kill me, you insensitive prick.*

Instead, Remo goes with, "Victor, I know, but—"

Victor cuts him off. "Got a lot of ink. Not favorable ink."

"They think I threw the case."

"Did you, asshole?"

"No, of course not. They also think I stole their money from the bank job."

Victor cracks a grin, speaks in a low, between me and you tone, "Did you, asshole?"

"No. My income clears seven figures by March. Why would I . . ."

"Don't get sensitive, just asking."

"What would I need the money for?"

Victor hits the down button for the elevator, thinking as he says, "Oh I don't know... booze, drugs? Snatch?"

"Victor, I think they're really going to try and kill me."

Victor stops, attempting to fake some concern. "Talk to the cops?"

Remo looks at him, incredulous.

"Sorry," Victor laughs, "They may shoot you themselves."

"I need protection."

"Call Hollis."

"You're full of fucking giggles this morning."

"He's the baddest man I know."

"We're not currently pals," recalls Remo.

The elevator arrives and they enter a car packed with workers from other floors. Remo and Victor slide to the back. Most people wouldn't think a public elevator is the best place to discuss matters such as this, but Victor and Remo aren't most people.

Victor continues. "That will happen when you fuck a hitman's wife . . . sorry, wives."

"Only fucked one wife," Remo responds.

The other elevator passengers alternate looking at the ceiling and their shoes. Wanting to get the point of this conversation, Remo asks, "Look, Victor, didn't Schmidt use a bodyguard service a couple of months ago?"

"Yeah, that gang shit-show went sideways and he needed a little looking after. Got him set up with this protection outfit, supposed to be the best in the city. Schmidt's still breathing, so . . ."

"Yeah, them. Set me up with them."

Earns an eyebrow raise from Victor.

"What?" Remo demands. "You want a please, cocksucker?"

More uncomfortable looks from their fellow elevator passengers.

Victor rubs his fingers together. "They ain't cheap, Big Fun."

"You're fucking kidding me, right? What was my number last year? Last month? Hell, last week—"

"Fine. Damn, you bitch a lot." Victor pulls his Blackberry, scrolls through a few things. "But Hollis is your best bet." He sends a text to Remo's phone, which buzzes. Remo reluctantly checks, finding a text that says HOLLIS, along with a phone number. Remo looks at it like Victor sent him a nude picture of his mother.

"He used to like you," Victor points out. "Make him like you again."

The elevator reaches Victor's destination floor as he pushes his way out. "Can we talk frankly for a second?"

Remo shrinks. "If we must."

"You've got demons. I know it and am fine with it because you always deliver. But when a Five Diamond criminal like Crow with a habit of killing hookers comes to me, concerned about you . . . Sweet fancy Moses, man, that should give you a moment of pause. Maybe dry out for a spell?"

Complete disbelief from Remo. "That's sweet, boss, but could you call the bodyguard before these animals eat my heart and make my corpse their girlfriend? Could I trouble you to make that fucking phone call?"

The elevator doors shut in his face in answer.

CHAPTER THIRTEEN

REMO SITS in an Irish pub across from a stern-looking wall of a man. His new bodyguard. Goes by Seck. They sit in uncomfortable silence as the place moves on around them. Remo tries to break the ice with some banter. "So, you from New York?"

"Yes." Seck likes the ice where it is.

"I'm from Texas originally."

Remo receives a blank.

"Little town you've probably never heard of."

Nothing.

Remo's working way too hard at this. "Tiny, tiny town."

Seck finally responds. "Mr. Cobb—"

"Thank God. You do know how to speak."

"Your firm is paying me to protect you. Keep you out of harm's way"

"That's the idea. "

"Keep you alive?"

"At the minimum," replies Remo.

"Right. That's what bodyguards do. We guard bodies. We are not escorts. This is not a date. If you're lonely, call somebody else. We understand each other?"

Remo smiles. "We're gold."

"Stupendous."

Seck and Remo move their conversation out onto lower Broadway. The client and his new bodyguard pass around and through the masses on the streets of NYC.

"Now, what's the issue with regard to your personal safety?" Seck asks as he scans for predators, checking reflections in the passing store windows, always on the job.

Remo tries to explain. "Nutshell, there's a few people running around who would like to kill me."

"Happens."

"Yeah, well, not to me. I mean, sure, there are a ton of folks walking the earth who don't really care for me, but they don't want to kill me. Not in a realistic sort of way, right? I'm sure plenty have entertained the idea of me dead, though none have actually gone this far. But I have it from a reliable source there is a particularly high threat level. I'm pretty certain someone will try to take me out in the very near future."

"Who's the source?"

"This dead Jesus-freak dude," Remo responds, in as matter-of-fact a way as he can. "Most guys find out they're dying from a doctor who starts off the conversation with, 'You've got a horrific disease.' Me? I get the 'Agitated psychos are coming to kill you' heads up. All from an ex-con neo-disciple of Christ who gets shot to shit while shoveling down fried rice—my fried rice."

"You don't need to worry, Mr. Cobb."

"Well, come on. Need to worry a little. Who doesn't worry when people are coming to kill them?"

Seck stops in the middle of the street and gives Remo a strong, reassuring look. "Mr. Cobb, I am the best at what I do."

Remo relaxes a bit, feeding off Seck's calm and confidence. He enjoys the feeling of security, thinks about how he's always taken that feeling—the feeling most people have pretty much all their lives, that they are safe going about their day-to-day business—for granted. Until now. He lets that feeling sink in, allows it to take hold.

With a nerve-shattering crack, part of Seck's head explodes.

Remo's new bodyguard wilts to the concrete, a decapitated flower. People scream while parting like the Red Sea. The street becomes a rippling wave of chaos. Remo ducks, fear tearing through every cell in his body.

No sign of the shooter anywhere, only people running for their lives. Remo rises to his feet, about to join the stampede, when he spots a man standing across the street. Stops dead.

Have I seen this guy before? Maybe. Fuck, have I? Remo can't place him, but of course the last time Remo saw him it was dark and the guy was wearing a bad beard, dark glasses, and a hoodie. This time he's able to get a good look at the youngest Mashburn.

Chicken Wing stands still among the bystanders scurrying for safety, staring directly at Remo. His mouth cracks into a bone-freezing grin, followed by a finger curl wave.

The blood drains from Remo's face as Chicken Wing gives a bounce-step and starts toward him. Chicken Wing walks a straight line through the masses running in every direction—a shark fin cutting through the water.

Remo takes off, pursued by Chicken Wing. He loves it when they run.

In and out of the crowds, they slice between gridlocked cabs, limos, and delivery vans. Remo darts in front of one of the few vehicles moving, a cab which stops just shy of taking off Remo's leg. He jumps, rolling across the hood, back bouncing hard off the windshield before tumbling back to his feet on the street.

Horns blare. Profanity flies. Chicken Wing's still on him. Remo cuts through Macy's, trying to find cover among the patrons long enough to catch his breath. Turning, looking, he doesn't see the man chasing him. Taking a beat, Remo works to gather his senses.

Chicken Wing springs through the store doors and scans the

floor, wild eyes looking for his unwilling playmate. Remo runs for all he's worth up the nearest escalator, Chicken Wing back in pursuit.

Second floor. Remo pushes and shoves his way through a Women's Sports Wear Sale, doesn't slow down or look back. His heart feels like it's pumping battery acid as he races to an exit door. He finds an employee-only stairway and takes the concrete stairs two, three at a time. Lungs on fire now, but he can't stop, flying to the emergency exit covered in alarm warnings. Remo pushes through, alarm screaming, and hits the street like he's shot from a cannon. Runs wild without knowing where he's going, only that he can't stop. The feeling of safety he soaked in just minutes ago gone as quickly as it came.

He spots a cab pulling out up ahead and chases it down, beating on the roof, slapping a palm to the window. The cab finally stops.

Remo dives into the back, a bona fide mess. Barely gets out, "Anywhere," to the cabbie before the cab door opens. Remo almost jumps out of his skin as Chicken Wing slides in.

"You mind if we split this? Got a flight to catch," Chicken Wing says with a shit-eating grin.

Remo can't speak. The cab takes off.

CHAPTER FOURTEEN

THE CAB CUTS through the packed New York streets where it can, weaving in and around traffic and civilians who are completely unaware of the situation playing out in the cab's backseat.

This is possibly the single most unnerving moment of Remo's existence. He's been in proximity to a lot of unpleasant individuals, no questions, but not like this. He's not completely sure it's number one, but sharing a cab with a psycho who murdered two people and intends to kill him is at least in the top three.

A silent ride, save for Remo trying to catch his breath, which isn't going too well. He keeps his eyes actively looking for an exit. Chicken Wing pulls a New York Times from the floor. They don't make eye contact. Remo labors to the get a hold of himself.

Chicken Wing breaks the silence. "Where ya headed?"

Remo can't believe the question, but he answers. "Away."

"Must be nice to have that kinda freedom." Chicken Wing puts the paper down and leans in close. Uncomfortably close.

"More freedom than you gave my brother."

Remo jerks back. "Stay the fuck away from me."

"I'm just saying." Chicken Wing goes back to the paper.

"Who are you?"

"You know me, man."

"Sorry, I don't."

"Friends and family call me Chicken Wing. To you, it's Mr. fuckin' Mashburn." Remo's blood stops. He's seen pictures, heard stories, but has never had the displeasure of meeting Mr. Chicken Wing Mashburn face-to-face.

The cab driver looks in his rearview, not liking where this conversation is going. "Everything okay back there?"

Chicken Wing says, "We're cool man. We're actors. I'm running through a . . . what's it fucking called? An improv. Isn't my buddy here good? Looks scared, doesn't he?"

The cab driver surveys them, says, "Yeah. You're pretty good, bro."

Remo's growing tired of Chicken Wing's bullshit, his little improv. "I don't know what you want, but—"

"Nothing really. Just the fucking money you stole from us. That's all. If you don't get us that, then we'll take your head. Your balls."

Remo beats on the separation between him and the driver. "Stop the cab."

The cab slows. Chicken Wing isn't interested in ending their talk. He beats harder on the glass. "No, good sir. Keep going, please." He turns to Remo. "You can't run away from this. You can try, but we'll find you." He flashes his .357.

"I didn't do whatever you think I did."

"No? Think about it good. Pretty sure you did."

"I don't have any of your money and I can't control the legal system. The judge ruled—"

"The attitude is unnecessary, dude."

Remo scrambles for something to say. "Okay, look. It wasn't supposed to happen like this. I've made mistakes."

Chicken Wing squeezes Remo's cheek, hard. "We're the sum of our mistakes, right? Dutch always says that shit. Lester shouldn't have come to you, and that bodyguard was unwelcome."

He lets go of Remo's cheek with a slap, leaving an outline of his fingers, a pinkish hue behind. Lester?

Remo suddenly realizes Chicken Wing was the guy in the hoodie. Pictures Chicken Wing's face with the bad beard and dark glasses, remembers the reckless violence. His memory is now crystal clear as he relives Lester spinning like a blood-soaked top on the floor of the Chinese joint.

Every part of Remo shakes.

The cabbie glances in the mirror again. "You really are pretty good."

Remo's eyes dart uncontrollably, scanning the streets. *What do I do?* The cab stops abruptly, inches from the bumper of a delivery truck, cabbie slapping the wheel in frustration. Now or never. Remo pushes the door open, exploding out into the street with arms and legs pumping like pistons firing. He pinballs through people crowding the streets but keeps moving, blocks passing in a blur. He reaches his apartment building in a balls-out sprint, flies through the lobby, and attacks the stairs two at a time all the way to his front door.

Pulling a leather duffel bag down from a shelf, he stuffs it like he was on the clock cleaning out a bank vault, cramming in items without any real thought or plan: socks, underwear, toothbrush, Q-tips...whatever he can find. He rifles through the closet, yanking ten-grand-a-pop suits off hangers and tossing them aside like they were last summer's Old Navy bargain graphic tees. He pulls down the last one, revealing a large safe in the wall.

Remo punches the code into the safe's digital keypad, and the door opens with a click.

Inside is a stack of cash. A nice stack of cash, sure, but nothing vaguely close to the 3.2 million the Mashburns are all hot and bothered about. Looks like a few grand, tops.

Remo pauses briefly. He takes a hard, thoughtful look at the blown out window from his recent gun experience. Yeah, that didn't go well. But this is one of the situations where it's better to be a well-armed idiot than an unarmed dead man. He yanks open his dresser drawer, grabs the Glock and stuffs it in the bag.

Remo rushes through the apartment building's subterranean parking garage, duffle over his shoulder. Clothes peek out from the bulging, unzipped bag. He tosses the bag into the passenger seat as he falls in behind the wheel of his Mercedes CL600. Remo pushes the ignition button, jams the shifter into D and speeds the hell outta there, the CL600 scraping the curb as it tears out of the garage.

Remo takes alleys at high speed, running rip-shit in and out of traffic—offensive driving at its finest. He makes New York cabbies seem tame and neutered in comparison. The Mercedes races across the Brooklyn Bridge, breezing past the other cars at a frantic pace, as if they were standing still. Escape and self-preservation are Remo's only concern as he taps nervously on the steering wheel, constantly checking the side mirrors. It's fight-or-flight in action, and flight has won by an overwhelming margin. Remo's been reduced to moving on instinct, and instinct is screaming to get the fuck out.

Peeling off an exit ramp, Remo's CL600 reaches a red light and comes to a stop. Remo's breathing is slowly but surely returning to normal. He's still on edge, but coming down a bit. He's bought himself some time to think about what the hell he's going to do. He tries to, anyway, but his thoughts are complete shit.

Who would know how to help me?

His mind drifts.

He grabs his iPhone and flips through it, eventually finding what he's looking for: a video he'd taken of Sean playing in the park.

He stares at the screen, almost through it. He wants to jump into the video and join that place—a place he gave up.

Remo stops just short of running his finger over the boy on the screen's hair. The boy is bursting at the seams with life, so happy, no sign of hate or anger. *What's that like?* wonders Remo. Can't remember ever feeling like that. Maybe he never did. He's transported to another world, a better world, where things make sense. This one makes no sense. Not now, not ever. Not Remo's world.

The light turns green and Remo's foot slides over, reaching for the accelerator . . .

Smash!

The driver's window explodes from the impact of a crowbar. It's a jarring moment of mind-bending confusion, punctuated by a fist crunching into Remo's jaw. He takes another blow to the jaw, then another that dots his eye. Spit and blood scatter. The hand now tugs at Remo's suit jacket, trying to pull him from the car. The seatbelt prevents Remo for being dragged from the car, keeps pulling him back into the driver's seat.

Remo thanks God for that.

A tactical knife comes in, sawing away at the seatbelt, through it. in seconds. The door's pulled open, spilling Remo out into the street where he rolls on the concrete. Fights to get his focus back, then he wishes he hadn't.

Above him stands Chicken Wing, .357 in hand. It's not aimed at Remo though, even though Chicken Wing would like nothing more than to execute this fucker right here and now. No, not yet. He holds the gun by the barrel.

Like a blunt weapon.

Remo knows what's coming as he mutters, "Sean . . ."

Chicken Wing whips the butt of his .357 into Remo's head.

LIVING A DREAM

PART III

CHAPTER FIFTEEN

THIS IS NOT REM SLEEP. This isn't even REMO sleep. This is what happens after a guy called Chicken Wing beats you to a pulp. There are no dreams. No tits, no pussy, and no aerial sex with a blue chick. There's only a thick, swollen mass of nothing.

A cerebral shit sandwich.

If there's a state of being wedged somewhere between awake, asleep and dead, this is it.

Remo drifts in and out of consciousness a handful of times. There's a flash of being dumped into a trunk and landing on a spare tire. He vaguely remembers not liking it. Later there was a red glow, of brake lights he guesses, flashing off and on while Remo rolled back and forth like a grocery sack.

Other than that bit of fun, all Remo knows is that it feels as if his skull was thrown down a hole, with demons and ghouls spitting on it all the way down. He also retains a smeared vision of Chicken Wing wailing on him, and noticing that Mr. Wing was really, really enjoying it. Remo can't wait for Johnnie Blue to take that memory out of his head. That is if he ever sees his good buddy Blue, or his favorite mix of R&B, again.

During one if his brief blips of consciousness, Remo thought he was going to die. For a fraction of a second, before he drifted off again, he thought that Chicken Wing was going to cut him up and spread his remains all over the city.

His eyes go heavy.

Roll back.

Back to black.

Remo comes back online again, remembers reading in the files that the Mashburns have done this bit before. They caught up with a witness, a cab driver who said something he shouldn't have...the truth. They hacked the guy into pieces with an axe and then fed those morsels, bones, guts and all, to some pigs down south.

He thinks it was in Georgia, maybe Arkansas.

Fortunately, Remo's been unable to maintain a consistent state of consciousness. Thank God for that. Not that Remo is a religious person at all, but where else is he supposed to go with this? He'd rather not watch the axe come down. Rather not be a treat for a pen of pigs. He'd rather just wake up later, in heaven.

That's right. Remo thinks he belongs in heaven. Fuck you for thinking otherwise. He feels the car slowing down. Remo's mind scrambles, screaming inside his head, *Please let me pass out again.*

The brakes squeak and the trunk lights up red as the car comes to a complete stop.

Remo's heart races, skipping beats, slamming harder and harder into his chest. His lungs can't find air. His mouth robbed of all moisture.

He can't tell if he's in his head or screaming out loud, but the message is clear: *Please. Help me. Please let me pass out now.*

A swollen, raw hamburger of an eye struggles to open. When it finally does, red spider webs decorate the white of his eye.

Remo is in a familiar spot: a stiff chair in his dining room. His face resembles road kill. His limp body hangs off the chair like a bachelor's laundry. Looking around, he's not sure how he got here. Sitting up, he scans his home, wincing the whole way. Even his hair hurts. Nothing is out of place, not a single thing moved, everything right as he left it. The front door is closed.

The leather bag he packed for his escape rests next to him. Even his baseball bat is against his chest, wrapped in his arms. He sees his customary bottle of scotch, a full glass on the table in front of him.

For a moment, he thinks maybe this isn't really happening. Like in the movies. It was a dream or he is dead—well, not that—or something along those lines. How sweet would that be? If all this shit was some big hoax his mind was playing. Or, maybe, he took a few too many whacks to the head from Chicken Wing and his brain crammed too far to one side or the other. Perhaps he had a few too many sips of the sauce and blacked out. Not like it's never happened. Perhaps he miscalculated his R&B and took a little snooze. That hasn't happened for a long time, but still, it's completely plausible. These thoughts bring him comfort until he moves the bat from his chest and finds a note pinned to his shirt.

Comfort shot to shit, he gives the note a rip. As he reads it his stomach sinks to the floor. His hands vibrate and his good eye twitches. Penned in the same writing, and skill level, as the previous note, it reads: *Told U not 2 fucking run cunt.*

Remo springs from his chair as a panic-fueled freak-out bubbles up and spills out. The chair flies backward, crashes hard against the wall, causing an overpriced painting to fall to the hardwood, breaking the glass.

He grabs the bat and searches the apartment. Races to the bedroom, yanks open the closet door. Empty. Heads to the bathroom, rips back the shower curtain.

Nobody. Back to the living room. Remo stumbles through. His eyes sink back into his skull. The weight of it all crashes down on him as Remo leans his back against the wall he slides down in a heap. Complete breakdown at his fingertips. He battles hard to keep it at bay. His options are complete shit, his life pretty much the same.

He looks to his iPhone on the floor. It lies there, mocking him, begging him to make the call. Almost slapping him with the obvious choice he needs to make.

Remo pulls up the text that Victor sent him earlier, the one with Hollis' contact info. This is the last call he ever wanted to make, but does it anyway. Like calling your parents for rent money when you've blown everything on booze, like asking your wife for one more chance, like asking someone you've wronged greatly to help save your life.

He dials. Each ring is like a vice grip to his testicles. Finally, there's an answer to his call of desperation.

A strong voice answers.

It's only one word, but it has a tone, a coolness that gives you nothing but tells you everything. The voice of Hollis answers, "Hello."

Remo has no idea how to start this conversation. Even the mere sound of Hollis' voice make him want to piss himself and hide under the table.

"Hello . . ." Hollis presses.

No choice. Remo swallows big and replies "Hollis, it's Remo."

Deafening silence from the other end of the call.

"Hollis, it's Remo. I don't know what to say here, but I need you to give me a minute . . ."

Click. Hollis is gone.

What little color Remo had in his face washes white as his thoughts do jumping jacks. He rocks back and forth, face wrapped in his hands. Pulls them away and stumble-crawls to the bathroom with as much speed as he can muster.

He flies to the bowl, flings up the lid, and vomits violently. It's the rare type of sickness that can only come from the knowledge that you will certainly die in a horrible, horrific fashion. From knowing it's all your fault and that things could have gone much, much differently if only...if only...

Fuck it. Remo falls back from the toilet, pulling down a towel from the rack.

Wipes his face and gives an oddly-timed laugh.

Deadman puking, he thinks with a giggle, a twinge of pain spiking up in every part of his body.

The cold reality of the situation hardens his expression. *I'm a dead man.*

CHAPTER SIXTEEN

THE LAST THING Lester remembers is really enjoying a handful of that delicious fried rice. Then there was the familiar crack of gunfire, some shattering glass, screams and then darkness. Now that he thinks about it, he recalls a flash here and there of an ambulance ride. There's also a fuzzy recollection of being rushed down a corridor by many people. Words and phrases like, "Not gonna make it," and, "Fucked," being thrown around.

As he opens his eyes and looks around, he realizes he's in a hospital room.

God bless them. He did make it. Lester scans the room with his eyes. He doesn't want to make any sudden moves that might draw attention or frighten the young woman checking his vitals. She's standing next to a tray that contains an array of medical things. He can't quite make out what they are. She's pretty, he thinks, real pretty. For a moment, in his weakened state, his mind reverts back to his old self. His old self would love a piece of this young, pretty nurse. His old self would do things, even if she didn't want to do them with Lester. He was inside for a long time —a long time without the touch of a woman.

He's only a man, he thinks, and man was born a sinner. What's the harm?

He allows his fingers to graze the young nurse's hand. She jumps back, more startled than anything, as she exclaims, "Oh my God!" The words, and the sweet sound of her voice, snap Lester back to a correct frame of thinking. Like a windshield wiper on his damaged psyche, his impure thoughts are wiped away.

His head gets right. The Lord. His new calling in life. Remo.

Lester jumps from the bed, tearing the tubes from his arms. He wraps his thick, tattooed hand around the nurse's mouth. Her eyes bulge as her voice is reduced to a muffled murmur under Lester's vice grip. He shushes her with a soft, caring tone. Reassuring her that he will not harm her, he just needs a few things and some information.

He speaks to her in a warm, friendly voice, barely above a whisper. "Blink once for yes, twice for no. Is there someone guarding outside?"

She blinks her green eyes once.

"Is he armed?"

One blink.

He moves her to the window so he can get a look outside.

The windows are sealed shut—he can work around that—it's more about the height. His room appears to be a few stories up. Nothing crazy, but still a long way down. Lester takes note of the ledge along the side of the building and a dumpster farther down the way, delivery trucks passing by. At least there are a couple of options. He won't know what will work best until he gets out there, but thank the Maker there are options.

Neatly folded in the closet are a pair of sweats and a nondescript white t-shirt. They must be there for when he wakes up and needs to go down to physical therapy. He takes a moment for personal inventory. Doesn't feel great, but he's felt worse.

He scans the tray the nurse brought in. It contains gauze, tape, and some syringes.

Again he addresses her in a kindly tone as he instructs, "Please take everything off that tray, and whatever you have on your person, and place it all in the trash bag from the bathroom. I have no intention of hurting you, but I will not hesitate to snap your pretty little neck if you prevent me from completing the Lord's work."

The nurse's heart pounds, reaching a level of fear she's only seen on TV.

Lester continues, "I also need you to assist me in changing into those clothes and dress my wounds for travel."

She's frozen. Terrified. Can't even muster a nod. Lester recognizes the symptoms. He's caused this response in men and women many times before. That was in the old days, of course. Perhaps he should have left out the "snapping her pretty little neck" bit. He's still learning to maneuver within his newfound faith. But, damn, it was easier in the old days. In those days he would simply resolve the situation with some violence. It would be quick and painless, for Lester at least.

No. While following his current path, the righteous path, he must stop and seek to understand what the other person is feeling. Seeking to understand is slow and somewhat painful at times, but it does keep a man in step with the Lord. This, for better or worse, is the path Lester has chosen.

Damn, it's hard work.

Lester takes a breath, forces himself back into his calming mode, and addresses her again. "Everything is going to be fine as long as we work together on this. Can you help me? Please blink once for yes, twice for no."

She starts to calm down. There's something in his eyes. She believes him.

Lester gives her the slightest of nods as if he's willing her, leading her to the correct answer.

She blinks once.

Lester hides his shock. That worked? Perhaps this isn't as hard as he thought. One last thing before they get started. He asks, "I had a bible with me. Do you know where it is?"

She blinks once. Good girl.

As if in slow motion, Remo drags his troubled bones through the streets.

The rest of New York City moves at its normal, infamous energetic pace, paying no attention to this guy who can't get out of first gear. They pass him by, moving around him like water rolling around a rock in its path.

It's all lost on Remo.

He walks down block after block, trying to piece together some plan of action. Aimlessly stares into shop windows. With glassy eyes, he watches as street performers and homeless do their thing. He doesn't even bother scanning for Chicken Wing.

Knows he's out there somewhere. *If he wants to kill me, I'm here.* While roaming, he passes a homeless guy holding a sign that reads, THE END IS UPON US. Remo stops in front of him, engrossed by the sign. His glazed stare is stuck on the words, as if not even reading them. More like he's studying the inside of his own head, and his eyes just have to look at something while he's doing it. His stare bores through the crude sign, all en route to a spot in his mind, a hopeless little corner of the universe that only Remo can see.

Homeless guy asks, "You okay?"

"No."

"World's on a freight train to hell, brother. You ready?"

The question—*You ready?*—sparks an idea in Remo. The answer is an overwhelming *No!,* But at the same time, Remo wonders why, if he can't stop his death, can't he at least be ready to die? Is that the way to look at this? Is that the angle to play? Like those movies where the character is told he has cancer or some shit and they go through a journey of self-discovery, blah,

blah, blah... yeah, those. Now, of course, Remo and self-discovery are like a porn star and virginity. You can't put the genie back in the bottle, but Remo chooses to look at it differently.

I'm going to die, and that sucks, but now what? What's the play? What's my move with this?

Remo's wandering has brought him to a coffee shop, where he's now sprawled out in a corner booth meant to seat six. A pot of hot coffee sits on the steel-topped table, his flask of Johnnie at the ready. Balled up wads of napkins are scattered among the salt and pepper shakers and the jelly tower. He works feverishly at writing something on a fresh napkin. He writes fast, pouring his mind out on the page, then stops. Crosses everything out and wads it up, tossing it to the side to keep company with the other scraps of ideas.

A young, hipster-punk waitress walks up, topping off his coffee. Tattoo sleeves wrap her arms and cover her neck. Mermaids or some shit. She could be very attractive, but damn that's a lot of ink. Nose and ears look like a pincushion.

She takes note of Remo's struggles with his writing, then asks, "Whatcha working on?"

Remo offers her nothing in the way of a response.

Undaunted, she tries again. "Looks like it's giving you some stress."

He pours from his flask into the coffee and spins it with a spoon, working to get the mixture just right. Takes a sip, adds some sugar. He'd rather not engage in conversation with this person. Drinking is a better way to spend his dwindling time on this earth.

"Oh come on, boss, I've been on since 3:00 a.m. You're the closest thing to interesting I've got." The waitress is almost begging him to engage. Remo can't take it. As if he doesn't have enough troubles, now he has to entertain this person with the remaining sand in his hourglass. He reluctantly replies, "List of shit I want to do before I die."

"Oh my God, are you dying?"

Remo covers. "No, no, heavens no. I'm good. I saw that damn movie the other night, you know the one? With the before-you-die list? I was flipping around, it got me thinking . . . not getting younger and whatever the fuck."

"Oh." She gives it a think, wondering what she would want to do before she bit the big one.

"Sunrise in Thailand?"

"No."

"Paris?"

"Could give a fuck."

"Three way with some black guys?"

"Look, I appreciate your input here. I do. But I don't have the kind of time for big-event type things."

The waitress pulls back, confused. "Don't have time? You said—"

"I mean, if or when you find out you're dying you don't have a lot of time to spend. In theory."

She gets it. "What would you do if you only had, what? A couple of days, maybe only a day left?"

"Bingo."

"I'd call my Mom."

Remo thinks, *dig deeper kid.* The waitress picks up a couple of the wadded up napkins.

"Well, what do you have so far?"

Remo tries to stop her. "Those are just notes."

"They all say, 'Meet Sean.'"

"Rough draft," says Remo, hiding the new napkin he's working on. He looks down the table so she can't see the tears forming in the corners of his eyes.

"I don't know you, but it seems to me if that's the one thing you have on a bucket list, then maybe you should go meet this guy. Who's Sean?"

Two words have never hurt more. "My son."

This is the first time Remo has said this to anyone. Sure, a lot of people knew, but Remo never discussed with anyone openly. Not with friends or co-workers or anybody. For some reason, at this moment in life Remo feels the need to share this with a complete stranger. All of this washes over Remo in an instant.

His first instinct is that he's losing it. Going soft in a moment of weakness. Then he realizes something, something so clear... something so clear that even this dumb-fuck with shit stuck in her face and retarded pictures drawn all over her body can see it.

The waitress gives an understanding nod, decides to share. "My dad left us when I was a kid, but I got this P.I. guy I was dating, well not really dating, more like a fuck-buddy situation... Anyway, he found my dad a year or so ago and I just haven't had the cojones to actually go see him."

As the waitress rambles on, her voice fades into the background noise. For the first time in days Remo's thoughts become focused—for the first time in a few years. The answer to at least part of his current dilemma has just become easily identifiable. Ideas fall in line behind his distant eyes.

He tosses a few bucks on the table, quickly leaving the booth, the waitress still yammering on as he pushes out the door.

CHAPTER SEVENTEEN

REMO ARRIVES at a downtown office tower. He plows through a floor filled with bustling cubicles in full swing, hunting for someone in particular. He looks like hell as he sticks his head in cubicle after cubicle with no success, rudely interrupting corporate drones from their tasks, coffee, and three-hour Internet breaks. A few get pissed, and a few more get really pissed. A dull murmur about the visitor buzzes around the floor.

One employee asks, "Can I help you, buddy?" Remo ignores him. Heads pop up like prairie dogs to get a look at the nuisance of the floor.

He checks the Men's Room.

Then the Women's Room, where he's met by a shriek and the inevitable, "Asshole!"

Across the floor. Anna sips coffee as she returns to her desk.

Anna is a naturally beautiful woman, with that rare light of happiness that seems to surround some people. It's a light that she can, and does, share. Some people have it. Not Remo, but some people. Not to say her life has been peaches and cream, not even close, but Anna is able to put things in perspective. Everybody has their baggage, their cross to bear and all that. But she's able to look at the world with big-picture mentality and understand that her struggles are nothing in the grand scheme of things. Through the years she's been able to gain a healthy view of life. She thinks having a child has helped her put things in their proper place. Sean is really what fuels her light.

Unfortunately, that light gets extinguished as she turns and notices Remo.

Her eyes widen, then harden at the sight of Remo disrupting the work day. She gets a sinking feeling, one she hasn't experienced in awhile. Anna never knew she had a bad side until she married Remo. He was a project, of course. Most women have one—at least one—they are convinced they can change, positive that the right woman can turn the guy around. They're completely certain there is a good, good man in there and that other people just don't see it like they do. Sometimes these women are right.

They never married Remo.

As Anna's eyes find Remo, her defense mechanism takes over. She drops down into her cubicle looking for cover, shrinking lower and lower as she hears the sounds of Remo on the hunt. She'd dig a hole under the cheap, carefully chosen corporate carpet if she could.

Shit.

This is her worst fear; this guy showing up at work. This motherfucker, here? Anna rarely resorts to f-bombs. Not that she judges those that do, it's just not her thing. Something about Remo turns her vocabulary into that of a hostile longshoreman.

She stands, closes her eyes, and finds the strength to utter a quiet, "Remo."

He doesn't hear her and keeps searching the floor like a man possessed. The entire company hates him by now. She swallows big, then tries in a louder voice. "Remo."

He stops a few rows over. The floor goes silent. Anna locks her eyes firmly on Remo.

Remo knows she's not happy to see him, but something in him melts all the same. It always did when he saw her. Even when he fucked things up, it never went away.

Remo says, "Anna. You look—"

"What..." she begins in a burst of anger. Noticing the entire company is watching, she pulls her rage back, begins again. "What do you want?"

"Can I have a word?"

"No."

"Just a few words. You can count them, then I'll leave." Anna would rather talk to a drooling mental patient armed with a chainsaw. With zero desirable options, she points toward a private conference room.

Remo stumbles, shoved into the conference room by Anna. The company's version of posh is decked out in bad art and a long, polished table surrounded by ten empty Herman Miller chairs. There's a projection screen at the far end of the room, with a ceiling projector just waiting to beam out PowerPoint genius. Anna slams the door shut.

Remo decides he should try to smooth things first by saying, "Now. I realize—"

Anna doesn't want to smooth anything. A woman scorned and ready to unleash. "What the fuck are you doing here?"

"It's good to see you Anna—"

"Oh, cut the shit, you complete fucking asshole. We agreed. The courts agreed. This . . . does not happen. No more drunk phone calls at three in the morning. No more just happening to bump into me on the street. No more motherfucking Remo."

Remo resets. "I understand I'm not your favorite person—"

"Did that just come out of your mouth? Are you fucking kidding me? Get out."

"I have to talk to you."

"No, you don't."

"No, really, I do."

"Really, you don't. Leave before I call security." She moves to a phone on the conference table and picks up the receiver. Remo scrambles for the best way to say what he needs to say.

"I'm dying."

Anna takes those words in, asks, "What?"

"I'm dying."

She puts down the phone. Sure she hates this guy, but doesn't want him dead—well, not literally. "How?"

"It's not important how, but I don't have a lot of time."

She collects herself, her thoughts, and finds her natural feeling toward her ex— animosity— resurfacing. "What the hell I'm I supposed to do with that information? You walk in here after years of shit and tell me, what, you're dying?"

"You're feeling mixed emotions, I get that."

"Fuck you," she paces. "Fuck you. Fuck you, Remo Cobb. Look at you. I can't tell if you're lying, dying or just looking for a pity blowjob."

"I'm not looking for a pity anything. I'm going to die. It's true. I just want . . ." He pauses, then says it. "I'd like to see Sean before I go."

Anna takes that like a steel-toe boot to the gut. In a way, she knew this day was coming. That some day he was going to want to meet their son. She hoped it wouldn't, but in the back of her mind she feared it. Carrying that fear just underneath the surface was her baggage, and her baggage was now standing in front of her.

"I'd like to at least meet the kid before I check out. Ya know?"

She fights the conflicting emotions pulsing through her. "You agreed to not be a part of his life, remember?"

Remo knows.

"You asked to not be a part of his life."

"I know what I said."

"We don't need you. We don't want you."

Remo recoils. "You hate me."

"You don't think I've earned the right?"

"Don't you think he would want to meet his dad?"

"I'm not even sure I believe you're dying."

"It's going to happen. Soon."

Anna's bitterness takes over. "He's already infected with your shit DNA. Nothing I can do about that. Do you really think I'm going to introduce you before you go away? Do you think I would do that to my son?"

Remo takes the hit. It hurts, and Remo's natural instincts kick in—to cut down whoever is in front of him. "Technically, *our* son."

Absolutely the wrong thing to say her.

"Please go away," Anna says, ice in her voice.

"Anna."

She looks to him, eyes begging. "Please, leave us alone."

"I only want to say hello to him."

She gives her final answer in the only way this guy will understand. "Remo, go away and die."

Her words cut, hurting even worse because he knows they were completely justified by the years of hurt he's caused, driven by all the things he's done to her.

To Sean.

It's a crushing moment of realization about the life he's carved out for himself.

He gathers the battered remains of the hope he had at the coffee shop, thinking he should have known better. It was a fool's errand while the clock is ticking on his final days, a waste of what little time he has left.

He gives an understanding, accepting nod to Anna as he exits.

Anna hates herself.

CHAPTER EIGHTEEN

A PRISON TRANSPORT bus rolls across a barren stretch of rural highway, which stretches like black arteries snaking through the land.

Steel mesh is bolted tightly to the security windows. It's just good old-fashioned, federally-funded transportation for psychos and sociopaths. Inmates are cuffed and secured to their seats. Not a word is spoken as they sway and bounce with the roads' imperfections.

Dutch Mashburn watches the world pass by, seemingly oblivious to what is about to happen.

Frank sits facing the inmates, his mind engulfed in an all-out war. He fights like hell not to show what's going to happen.

What he's going to.

What he has to do.

The battle's raging in his head—right vs. wrong, and all the wrong that will happen to his wife if he doesn't make things right with Dutch. He grips a shotgun, wipes the sweat from his brow. Wrong has an impressive win/loss record.

Dutch turns to Frank and flashes a look.

It's time, shitbird. Frank knows it's time. Every part of him hates it, but these animals have his wife. Memories of how they met, hot dates, all of their special times together, spiral into and mix with his overactive imagination's ideas of what they might do to her.

Pushing aside his internal struggle, he takes to his feet and moves down the aisle, passing inmate after inmate. Frank takes them in as he passes with unsteady steps. The choices they've made, they all deserve to die. *Fuck 'em,* he thinks. His wife doesn't deserve this. He doesn't deserve this.

The portly bus driver checks his rearview, taking in the monster cargo behind him.

Frank reaches Dutch.

They share a silent moment. It's all over Frank's face; he's losing his will to do this. Dutch's granite-gaze coupled with a mocking slash to the neck reminds Frank that his wife will die if he's not helpful, as in right fucking now.

"Everything all right back there?" asks the bus driver.

Dutch's hate-drenched eyes slip to him then back to Frank. "You going to answer him, asshole?

"Yeah, it's fine," replies Frank. He pulls a set of keys, turning his back to the driver.

Frank speaks, low and shaky. "Look in my eyes and tell me she's okay."

Dutch smiles. "What do you think I am?"

Dutch knows something Frank doesn't. He knows that not far from here Ferris is exiting Frank's home, getting into a stolen roofers' van and driving off. Ferris will check his watch. Count to five. Then Frank's house, along with his little lady, will burst into a fireball. Dutch is more than comfortable knowing all this—actually hasn't given it a lot of thought up until now. Of course Frank knows none of this as he locks eyes with Dutch, otherwise Frank would blast that shotgun into Dutch's smiling, knowing face.

Frank thinks he has no other play here, so he unlocks Dutch's cuffs and chains. Stepping back, he gives Dutch a silent finger count.

One . . . Two . . . Three.

Frank calls out for the benefit of the other guard and the driver. "Sit down, Dutch!"

Dutch springs up, locking his arm around Frank's throat, twists his shotgun away. The other guard gets up, trying to level his sidearm.

Blam!

Dutch drops him, blood spray hitting the roof and front row of prisoners.

"No!" screams Frank. The site of his fellow guard being blown away, because of him, is almost too much. Because he was trying to save his wife, this guard will not be going to his home. Frank pushes that reality to the background, rationalizes something about how we all know the risks, and that's the job.

Inmates scream and cheer like it was NFL Sunday.

“Pull over,” Dutch instructs the driver, calm as can be. The driver's eyes bounce between his rearview mirror and the road. Dutch fires a shot into the roof.

The driver yanks the wheel, pulling over to the side of the road. $30k a year ain’t worth it. Sure, dental’s nice, but fuck it. He’s been thinking of going back to school anyway.

The bus is now complete chaos, escalating by the second. Rocking, bouncing and swaying, shocks and struts put to the test by the inmate's pent-up bloodlust. Still fastened to their seats, they tug like rabid animals whipped into a full-blown frenzy. They beg Dutch to set them free, calling out to him as if he's their Lord and Savior. He ignores their pleas, pushing Frank to the front of the bus.

“Open the cage,” orders Dutch. The driver looks to Frank, then Dutch. “Open that door or I kill him and release the freaks on you.” Again, the math is simple—not worth the trouble. The driver opens the cage door and Dutch pushes Frank through.

Without a second thought, Dutch delivers a shotgun blast into the driver's face.

A roar from the fans in the cheap seats.

Dutch shoves Frank out the bus's doors, where he rolls into the dirt, reduced to a puddle of emotion. Through rage-induced tears Frank calls out, "We had a deal."

Something catches Dutch's eye; a roofers' van speeding their way.

"We did."

"You won't hurt her?"

"I won't."

The van pulls up, driver's window lowering to reveal Ferris at the wheel.

"Or me?" asks Frank.

"I won't," sneers Dutch, as Ferris fires two .357 slugs into Frank's forehead.

Frank's body hasn't even hit the ground when Dutch enters the van.

The reunited Mashburns speed off, leaving in their wake three dead prison guards and a busload of Satan's minions, still strapped to their assigned seats. The bus jolts in every conceivable direction, like it was a sack full of wild monkeys trying to fuck a football.

Dutch sits back, letting the wind blow through his rat's nest of hair. Ferris steals a quick look at his brother, allows a small smile, but says nothing.

Hands Dutch the .357.

CHAPTER NINETEEN

REMO'S PACE is that of a dead man walking. Void of any form of expression, his facial muscles hang from his skull. Throngs of busy people rush along with a vibrant pulse that matches their city, while Remo moves at a crawl.

You couldn't find his pulse with a map. He's a man who has given up, accepted his fate. Accepted what the Mashburns are going to do to him and that he can't do a damn thing about it. He remembers the pictures and reports from the numerous assaults and murders the three brothers have committed over the years: blunt force trauma, strangulation, decapitations and—when they're feeling their Christian side—gunshots. All these thoughts and more string together at random, coming together in a collage of introspection.

Do I deserve to be alive? What do I have to offer this place? Not a whole helluva lot.

Church bells ring in the distance. There's a Catholic cathedral a few blocks over. Remo's not exactly a man of tremendous religious discipline. However, he does acknowledge his Southern Baptist upbringing—which is to say that his grandmother dragged him to the Lord's house while his daddy slept one off. They had snacks. He remembers a wad of bread and shot of grape juice. And not to be a dick, but isn't church where people go when they're dying? Where normal people go in an attempt to make peace with the man upstairs before they check out? That kinda thing?

Remo crosses the street, heads in that direction.

A hundred or so men and woman, all dressed in black, stand waiting as a casket is shepherded out of an elegant hearse. He can't keep from watching the polished oak casket moving along. The care the pallbearers give to it. The care they all share for whoever's inside that box. It's pretty damn moving when you think about it—that thing looks fucking heavy.

Remo enters the magnificent house of worship. Stained glass fires off striking beams of colored light. An organ produces a rich soundtrack, letting you know it's okay for sadness; it's okay for tears. This is where you grieve. So, please, grieve.

He takes note of the sorrow on the faces of the people paying their final respects to their fallen friend or family member. His body tightens, eyes watering. Not for the poor soul in the handcrafted wooden box; he doesn't know that man or woman. Nor are his tears for the loved ones left behind to pick up the pieces from this person's passing.

Remo's sadness is for himself. He sees the truth of his life, and it hurts. There will be nothing like this when he bites it. Not even close.

An elderly man passes and Remo grabs his arm to stop him. "Yes?" asks the man.

"How did you know the deceased?"

The man delivers his answer with great warmth, from a special place in his heart. The wrinkles in his face loosen above his glowing, honest smile. Just talking about the departed seems to melt years off the man. "He was a great friend to me and my family for years. I've known him a long time—"

Remo cuts him off. "You're going to miss him?"

The question confuses the man. "Terribly."

Remo moves on, stopping other funeral guests as he goes.

Finds a young woman and asks her, “And you, you’ll miss him as well?”

“Of course, he was—”

Not needing the full answer, Remo drifts on, moving to another, and then another. He’s beginning to cause a scene at the funeral he’s crashing. People are staring, starting to take note of the strange and disheveled man asking about the deceased.

Remo’s mind is an emotional taco salad, trying to balance the idea of this amazing mass of people gathered to honor the life of someone they cared about deeply against the crushing reality of the certain, nasty death he’s facing.

The church begins to swirl and twist, the world crashing. He shuffles in no clear direction, speech reduced to the muttering of a crazy person. For a moment he turns in a slow, small circle. He’s made it completely around the church, back around to the first elderly man, who stops Remo and asks, “May I ask whom you are?”

Remo ignores him, asks the older man the question of Remo’s lifetime. “And when you get your ticket punched, old-timer, people will probably miss you too?”

The old man’s answer is simple and so clear. “I hope so.”

Those three words put Remo’s mental puzzle together, slamming the pieces in place for the first time. People will miss the old man, no need for him to hope so. Remo knows he needs more than hope for people to miss him. In fact, nobody will miss him when he dies—sorry, when he gets viciously killed and left as a bloody mess for wild pigs to feed on.

He’s built an impressive portfolio of reasons for people to not only not miss him, but rejoice when he dies. Hell, they might throw a parade.

Fuckers.

Sure, a few criminals will miss his legal services, but fuck those guys. Really? *That's it?* he thinks, *that's the sum of me?* Uncharacteristically, Remo hugs the man for an extended period of time, hoping maybe some of the old man's good nature will rub off on him. Perhaps the proximity of good people will help. Can't hurt. But even the kind old man has his limits. "Could you please release me, son?" Remo drifts out of the church, all eyes on him. No longer kind, understanding eyes, these are the eyes of men and women who have now joined the long list of people who don't want anything to do with Remo. He wants to thank them, but we're past that now. Remo slips out the door, making the long, lonely walk to his deluxe apartment in the sky.

CHAPTER TWENTY

THERE'S a song that rattles around in Remo's head from time to time.

He avoids it when he's sober. When he's hammered, he gives it a listen. By the time the last chords of the song fade away Remo's usually in a puddle. It's an obscure Pink Floyd song from one of their lesser-known albums.

The song is "The Final Cut."

It lasts four minutes and forty-nine seconds.

There's no chorus or catchy riffs to speak of, but the lyrics?

The words, man.

Those words, Roger's, they cut right through him every damn time.

Tonight Remo is drinking like a boss with "The Final Cut" worming deep into his busted brain. Roger's words are moments away from sending Remo down for the count.

A gulp of booze.

A flood reaches the eyes.

Down goes Remo.

CHAPTER TWENTY-ONE

REMO SITS stone-faced in his apartment, the ever-present glass of scotch in hand while seated at his long, empty dining room table. It's imported from... somewhere. He remembers that someone referred him to a gay guy who hand-picked everything in the place. Nothing here has any real meaning or history, other than Remo's memory of suffering through the gay guy's presentation of his urban chic vision.

Remo's set up a small video camera on a tripod on the far side of the table, lens pointed directly at him. A one-man press conference of sorts.

He looks long and hard into the camera's lens, struggling to capture his thoughts before starting this little exercise. Maybe this was a bad idea.

No, it is a good idea. Great idea. Just fucking do it already.

He clears his throat, starts to address the camera. Stops for a snort of scotch. Coughs and clears his throat again.

Shakes his head hard side-to-side and then starts. "Boy . . . Son . . . Sean. You have no idea who I am, and that's probably a good thing." Thinks, then goes with it. "I'm your dad."

Takes a beat to let that sink in. Sounds funny for him to hear.

No one ever talks to him about Sean, and God knows he never talks about Sean to anyone else. Well, aside from the goofy waitress. He can't imagine what it will sound like to Sean.

Remo continues, "I set up a college fund for you, started it when you were born. Your mom doesn't know about it. You should go to school, drink . . . drink a lot. It'll assist in the realignment of your thinking about your old man."

Sip of scotch.

"You should drink and get weird with a lot of girls. Everybody says that kind of behavior doesn't help; they're fucking idiots. It helps. Helps a lot. Sorry, off topic."

Gulp of scotch.

"My sperm donor of a daddy died in a shootout. Unfortunately, it's looking a lot like your's might bite it the same way. His was for cheating an unfriendly poker game. Mine is, well, slightly more complicated. Same error in judgment, I suppose... fucking drifting again. Sorry, man."

Another gulp. Pours more. "You're going to hate me for a long time and you won't really know why. That's okay. I should have been around to show you shit, I know I should have."

He pushes the glass away and pops open his pill bottle, scattering out a few on the table in front of him. Preparing.

"You got good DNA kid, no question. Your Mom's a MILF, and I'm not bad either. Both of us are pretty bright bulbs, so that has to put you ahead of the curve. Good-looking and smart goes far in this life. Sucks for the armies of hideous dumbasses that clog the planet, but it is a fact. People will like you, and definitely will want to show up to your funeral. That's a long way off, but it's important."

Takes a mouthful of scotch, swishes it side-to-side before a hard swallow. He picks up a pill, getting it ready between his thumb and index finger.

"You should live like you want people to miss you. There, that's a good one. I'll leave you with that bit of wisdom."

He bounces the pill, trying to land it in the scotch glass.

"Take it easy on your mom. Take care of her. She deserved a helluva a lot more than me. . . as do you. Just know that I think of you frequently. I've set aside some things for you. Your mom will know what to do. But Sean . . ." Remo's eyes water, but he holds it together. "All of this—me talking here, the mindless babbling—this is really me trying to say, in an extremely piss-poor fashion, that I'm so very, very sor—"

His ringing cell phone cuts him off in mid-sentence. Plop. Finally got one in the glass. Remo sees the caller ID, answers with a confused, "Hello?" Nothing on the other end.

"Anna?"

Anna clutches her cell, standing in the doorway of her homey kitchen. Unlike Remo, she picked everything out by herself.

Sean sits coloring a *Toy Story 3* picture at the table. Woody and Buzz are an odd mix of magenta and periwinkle, but the kid's enjoying himself. Anna tries hard to keep her conversation with Remo away from Sean. "Remo, I shouldn't have said those things. You deserved every word and it was the truth, but I shouldn't have said them. Are you really dying?"

Remo, touched, replies, "Unfortunately."

"Let's be clear, I will never forgive you."

"Understood."

"Stop. Let me talk. I don't like this, and I'm certain this is a massive mistake, but... you should meet Sean. If I don't let him meet you, I'll hate myself later." The conversation is emotionally exhausting for her.

For first time in a long, long time, a light shines in Remo. "Thank you, Anna."

She can hear in his voice that he means it. At least, she'd like to think he's being honest. She snaps, "No talking. I'll meet you Saturday at seven. They're doing a thing for kids at the park that night."

Remo doesn't want to make a mistake with this. "Help me out. I haven't checked a calendar in a few days."

"Today is Friday."

"Okay. Yes. Absolutely. I'll be there."

"Remo... don't fuck this up."

"No. No way. I will be—"

She hangs up.

Remo looks straight into the camera, "There."

Wipes the moisture from his eyes.

Sniffs.

"Well, okay then."

He gives a grin, his heart wide open.

His expression shifts as his mind clicks, data churning. A thought comes to light, and he hates himself for not piecing this together sooner, pissed that this is something he should have realized long before. *Why haven't they killed me yet? Chicken Wing could have easily done it by now, so why hasn't he? He can't!*

It's a fucking family dynamic issue, some bizarre organizational chart Mashburn chain of command.

He can't do anything until his brothers get here. Remo shuts off the camera and hustles out. His beloved pill sits at the bottom of the glass, dissolving into granules swirling in good scotch.

CHAPTER TWENTY-TWO

REMO SCOURS the aisles of a late night convenience store. He checks his new best friend, the Glock he's tucked in his belt for safe keeping. Checks it just about every five seconds, like a newly married man twists his wedding ring after the ceremony—some things you have to get used to.

He hunts down the aisles, searching for something specific, even though he doesn't even consciously know what he's looking for.

Finally, he finds the goal of his hunt in the aisle of random crap packed high with gaudy tourist bait—worthless Made-in-Taiwan NYC souvenirs—there to amaze the taste-challenged. Remo wonders, *who buys this shit?* He picks up a Statue of Liberty, checks the weight. That's not it, but close. Puts it back, lifts a marble ashtray with a cheaply painted silhouette of the Brooklyn Bridge. He thinks this could be the one; it's heavy.

Likes it.

He continues his shopping, finding a generic white electrical extension cord. Takes two.

Outside the all-night convenience store, a late-model battleship of a black Lincoln sits parked across the street, Chicken

Wing behind the wheel. He studies the store. The streets are almost vacant at this wee hour of the night. He inhales a bag of peanut M&M's as he watches. He's surrounded by a landfill of empty candy bags, Big Mac boxes, wadded up Taco Bell wrappers, crushed coffee cups, and a piss jar. Chicken Wing is on a stakeout, and fucking hates it. If it were up to him, and it's not, he would have already cut that lawyer's head off and mounted it above the fireplace of whatever house in wherever the fuck country Dutch was talking about blowing away to after they get their money. Chicken Wing allows his broken mind to imagine this unknown country. A place where he can be himself, free of all the shit that holds him back (meaning laws and his brothers), and of course a place filled with hot women who have no other desire than to please Lord Chicken Wing. What a glorious place it will be.

In lieu of that special place, Chicken Wing has been stuck in a Lincoln for days with shit grub, forced to peer through binoculars, watching this fucking cocksucker Remo like some half-assed stalker. Though it has been fun to watch Remo as he comes mentally undone. Chicken Wing has seen all of it. The zombie strolls through the city. The hanging out in the coffee shop. And, of course, that little show at the funeral. That was a good one.

His burner cell goes off.

He answers. There's no "hello." No "thank you for all you've done." No appreciation for the fact he's been pissing in a jar. All that comes his way are questions, with a hearty helping of attitude.

He fucking hates it.

Bites his tongue, answering, "How the fuck should I know what he's doing? Shopping for the Last Supper."

In the stolen roofers' van, Ferris mans the wheel while Dutch talks to his little brother. Dutch and Ferris have had their differences, sure, what brothers don't? But they share a singular philosophy on how to deal with Chicken Wing. You must be clear, be precise, and if he fucks up, be harsh.

"Do not kill him," says Dutch.

Annoyed, Chicken Wing responds, "You fuckers keep telling me that. I. Fucking. Know." He gets more worked up with each syllable. "All the fucking time with you people."

"Calm down."

"Fuck you, calm down." Chicken Wing sees Remo exit the store. "Wait. He's coming out." Remo makes a beeline toward the Lincoln with his bag of goods from his shopping spree.

"He's coming this way."

"Why?"

"He's crossing the street, coming toward me." Remo pulls out the Brooklyn Bridge ashtray as he gets closer to the Lincoln.

"What's he doing now?" asks Dutch.

"Fuck!"

Remo pulls back the ashtray, giving it a major league heave at the driver's side window. The old school Lincoln's window shatters, a buckshot of glass shards bouncing around the interior, covering the huddled Chicken Wing.

The sounds from the other end of phone earn a look of deep concern between Dutch and Ferris.

Remo works quickly. Chicken Wing scrambles and Remo smacks his Glock across Chicken Wing's jaw, which makes a satisfying pop and crunch.

Damn, that felt good, thinks Remo.

Once more he whips the gun into Chicken Wing's face. Hell, does it again. The release of violence is intoxicating.

"You lost your fucking mind?" Chicken Wing calls out with a spit of blood.

Remo gives him another smack, enjoying it a little too much. "I'm calling your bluff." He grabs the extension cords from the bag.

"I'll kill you. I swear to fucking God." Chicken Wing thrashes with rage.

"You can't or you would have done it already, right boy?"

Chicken Wing is dazed. Bleeding. Pissed.

Remo continues his work, wrapping Chicken Wing's hands tight with the extension cords, just like he learned in Cub Scouts —knew it would come in handy someday. "Big brothers won't let you. That has to suck for you." He takes the second cord, tying it around Chicken Wing's neck. Remo sees his cell on the seat, grabs it. "That you, Dutch?"

“Hello, Remo.”

Chicken Wings struggles to get loose; it’s a lost cause. Remo clutches the phone. “You want me, come get me. You’ll hear from me by sundown with the location. This all stops. You hearing me, you fuckin’ faggot?” Remo knows from years working with the criminal element that you can say a lot to these guys and it will roll off their backs, but “faggot” usually gets their attention.

The street is silent save for Chicken Wing fighting the cords that bind.

Dutch finally answers, “Yes, Remo.”

“I’m dumping your brother at my place, pretty sure you know where it is.” Remo jams the cell in Chicken Wings shirt pocket. Chicken Wing groans some inaudible, profanity-laden threat.

Remo gives him another pistol-whip, just for good measure, and for fun.

A nice, tooth-removing smack from the Glock’s Nylon 6.

Remo's cab pulls to a stop in front of a gorgeous home nestled in a suburban golf community. Yard’s manicured to absolute perfection. A dog barks in the distance, more than likely a pure-bred. A marriage of two Lexus in the drive: one SUV, one sedan. A very cute couple.

Stepping out from the cab, Remo looks over the place. His face hardens, neck muscles tighten. Something in that pleasant, inviting home has him scared shitless. He hands the cabbie a wad of sweaty cash, and the yellow cab peels off, roaring past the rows and rows of comfortable homes.

Remo takes a moment for personal inventory. *I don't want to do this, but do I have a choice?*

Nope.

He makes the seemingly endless death march up the shrub-lined walkway, making note of the lovely rose bushes along the way. He dodges a basketball sporting a Knicks logo before reaching the two thousand dollar, handcrafted front door that was designed to look old and worn.

Remo takes a deep breath, says a small prayer, and rings the doorbell.

Inside, a sculpted soccer mom goes to answer. Jenny, as she's known around the neighborhood, works hard to maintain and improve the genetic gifts she's been given. Her looks and the appearances that come with the zip code help to hide the truth: Jenny has a past.

It is precisely that, though. Her past.

Children whining in the background, she grabs the door handle. "Just a second, I've got to get the door."

She checks the peephole, sees Remo. "Fuck me," she says just under her breath.

On the other side of the door Remo, knows what she's probably thinking, says, "I understand you have no good reason to open this door."

A man walks up behind her and puts a strong, reassuring hand on Jenny's shoulder. He's got this. She would like to open the door and kick Remo in the nuts, but she's not that girl anymore. Instead, she walks off to tend to the children.

The man is dressed like your average dad: king of the burbs, master of the cul-de-sac. Carries the looks of a successful engineer who jogs and maybe plays tennis. Definitely plays golf. But please, make no mistake . . . he's not that guy.

Hollis is a bad, bad man, and if you force him to demonstrate that, you will not like the show.

Remo continues talking, thinking Jenny's still guarding the gate. "I really, really need to talk to him."

"What do you want, Remo?"

Remo starts squirming, the sound of Hollis's voice pushing pause on Remo's heart. All of their history, good and shitty, comes rushing to him. It's the shitty that really has Remo concerned.

He utters, "Five minutes, friend."

Hollis wraps his large hand around the knob, gripping it tight. He almost feels the steel start to dent in his grip as his knuckles go white. He's reviewing the shitty as well. Hollis throws open the door and barks, "Two words: 'fuck' and 'no.'"

Remo jumps back, says, "You know I wouldn't come here if I had any other choice." He gives the most sincere eyes he can muster. "Please, man."

Hollis locks onto Remo, cocks his head, trying to read the most impossible man on the planet to trust. "You get three minutes."

Remo tries to step through the door but Hollis stops him cold, planting his meaty palm in the center of Remo's chest. "Not a single damn toe in my house. Back yard."

The door slams in Remo's face, yet he can't help but feel hopeful. Considering Hollis didn't rip his heart out or stomp his skull on the front porch, this is a positive sign.

Remo enters the sanctuary of the backyard through a wooden gate. Hollis waters his numerous rose bushes with an 8-Pattern, pistol-grip spray nozzle. He's chosen a fan spray setting for his rose's soil; it works the best. The care he takes is obvious. Hollis refuses to make eye contact as Remo cautiously steps in his direction. Remo's smart enough to leave some space between them, a comfort cushion.

Over the years, Remo has found it's best to open a conversation with something that makes the other person comfortable. Something that will perhaps form a bond between them, or at the very least break the icy landscape that separates them, hopefully planting the seeds of a new, stronger relationship—one that Remo can manipulate for his own wants and needs, of course. In this case, Remo goes with a comment about the man's flowers. "It's really coming together—"

"The pair of balls on you is beyond comprehension," Hollis fires off.

"You're upset, perfectly understandable."

"Appreciate that."

"But I did keep you out of ten-year jail stretch."

"You also fucked my first wife, got a handjob from the second, and tried to work a three-way with the third."

"You could thank me for saving you from those first two whores. That third one in there, though, she's a real catch."

"Two minute warning." Remo's on his heels in this discussion. Scrambling, he replies, "I've got nowhere to go with this. You're it, I'm sorry. I wish I didn't have to come here today, but I'm fucked, man. People are coming for me."

"Shocking."

"Bad men are coming to kill me and they will be monumentally successful unless you help me. You're the only one who can throw me an assist here. Please. Come on... save me. It'll do your soul a solid."

"Final minute."

"I can't fight these people alone, you understand? I will be dead. I can't run from this. . . fucking tried." His voice cracks, a slight chink in his armor that doesn't go unnoticed by Hollis, who continues to water the nicely kept rose bushes.

Still zero eye contact.

Remo continues to pour his heart out. "I'd like to live, Hollis. I'm working toward being a slightly better human."

Hollis turns off the spray. "And we're done."

The hose drops.

Remo drops the shit, digs out the truth. It's hard for Remo to find, given that he's spent the majority of his life avoiding truth of any form or fashion, has made a fortune slicing the truth up, throwing it in a blender with some bullshit alteration of the facts, then shoving it down your throat with a big smile.

Remo fumbles, but finds the heart of the matter. "I have a kid, a son, I abandoned. I turned my back on him." Remo sees he has Hollis's attention and keeps going. "I've done countless shitty things. Helped a lot of shitty people get away with shitty things . . . immeasurable moments I wish I could undo, but I can't. I can, however, maybe, just maybe, salvage something from this waste of sperm and egg I've turned out to be. I'm trying man. I'm trying hard to do the correct thing."

All defenses are gone, a raw nerve of a man. "I've been bold, now I need a mighty motherfucking force to come to my aid. Please help me."

Hollis finally looks in Remo's direction, sizes up the moisture building in Remo's weary eyes. He hates everything about this man. He can't help but glance at his kids through the window. They are fucking up the house, and Jenny's screaming at them, but they are his kids, and the love he has for them is immeasurable. Hollis remembers when his first was born. Something in him shifted; there was an actual change in his thoughts and feelings.

That change didn't happen when Jenny told him she was pregnant—a call he took mere minutes after executing five mid-level targets in Bangkok. No, it didn't register until he was waiting for the nurses to bring him into the delivery room. He was alone, dressed in scrubs, waiting for his first child to be born, and all he could think about was how he needed to take care of family. Even thought about changing his line of work. Of course, that didn't happen. Look, he's in his forties and he does what he does. He can't go back to school or start a new trade, go entry-level at some crap company for 30K a year with bennies after the first 60 days. Not when he makes high six figures in bad years, seven in the good ones. No, now he just makes better decisions about the jobs he takes.

Hollis is a first-rate killer. A global, all-star, motherfucking murder man. He's killed in hot, cold, and room temperature blood, dropped bodies on every continent, and told people they were going to die in more languages than Rosetta Stone can teach. But even he can't ignore what he sees in Remo.

"Meet me at Chili's."

CHAPTER TWENTY-THREE

CHILI'S. That bundle of glory that is Middle America's home for fine dining. Hollis sits across from Remo in a booth toward the back, a location Hollis has selected so he can view all entry and exit points, as well as keep a good line of sight on the kitchen. Just in case some fucker decides to come out blazing.

A table tent separates the two of them, proudly displaying a dizzying array of colorful drinks and towering dessert options, all for reasonable prices. Rarely is there this much tension at a Chili's, but there's been nothing but stares and uncomfortable silence between them since they sat down. Remo can't take it anymore, opens up the conversation by saying, "I can't begin to describe how much this means to—"

Hollis can't take it either. "Asshole." Hollis stops while a young waitress drops off a plate of appetizers with zero zest for life. When the abruptly delivered plate stops sliding, Hollis continues. "I haven't agreed to a damn thing. Now, what are you proposing here?"

"Bluntly speaking, we gotta kill these fuckers. Going to be three of them--"

"Probably more," Hollis states matter-of-factly, based on his extensive experience with this type of situation.

"Sweet Christ, I hope not. You think so?"

"You defended these guys?"

Remo shrinks. "Kinda."

"Care to expand on that?"

"I was going through a bit of a time during their case. The wife left me—"

"Smart girl."

"Without question. I fell into a little depression, self-loathing. The descent dumped me into the abyss, and then this case comes to me. Could have won it fair and easy; cops fucked up everything. But I couldn't do it. I've seen a ton of horrible things over the years, but this one...man. They shot everybody. Most were unarmed, face down. There was this woman and her kid. Kid ... a baby, really." Remo drifts, comes back. "They shot everyone."

Hollis watches, trying not to show sympathy for this complete waste of oxygen sitting across from him. Keeps listening as Remo goes on. "I threw the case."

Hollis's eyes go wide. "Sweet, counselor."

"That's not all. They got away with just north of three million. As their attorney, I told them I needed to know where it was stashed."

There it is, thinks Hollis, *fucking knew it.* He starts to reassess being here.

"I dug up the money," Remo confesses.

"Give it back."

"Don't have it."

That does it for Hollis. "I'm leaving." He begins sliding out.

Remo scrambles to keep him there by saying, "I didn't want that money landing with the cops, going wherever the fuck it happens to go. I gave it all away. One hundred percent."

"Where?" asks Hollis.

"I gave it to the foundation they set up for the families of the bank victims."

Hollis knows better. "You lying fuck."

"Why doesn't anybody believe me? I gave it away. Seriously, I did. Roughly ninety percent of the money went to them."

Hollis flicks aside a Loaded Potato Skin, grabs a Southwestern Eggroll. His disbelief wrapped in disapproval spins round and round. He busts into a series of uncontrollable laughs.

"Not funny. Not funny at all."

"Oh, it is. The one vaguely decent thing you've done with your miserable life is the thing that's going to get you killed." Hollis is now rolling with laughter. "Classic. I'm so glad you stopped by today."

"Glad I helped you find your smile."

"Simply awesome."

Remo tries to ignore his "buddy's" enjoyment of the situation. "I've got a vacation home in East Hampton. It's secluded, nobody else will get hurt. They think I'm handing over the money. Told them I'd call by sundown."

"What are you, Wyatt Earp?"

"So what I propose," Remo continues, ignoring Hollis' sarcasm, "is you, guns, and a pile of dead fuckers. Name your price."

"I'm not going anywhere." Hollis stuffs the once-discarded potato skin in his mouth as he starts to slide out again. Remo's heart drops, his last bit of hope fading away. He has no other plays left. That's it. It's all over.

It's really fucking over.

Hollis turns back to him. "I'm going to the mall. You in or not?"

Remo follows Hollis as he strolls among the suburban shoppers in a mall that buzzes with parents, teens and children, as well as some elderly people using the place as a walking track. A 1,434,786 square foot monument to disposable income and the American dream.

Hollis stops at a large window outside a Gap, admiring a sweater.

Remo is beyond anxious. "No offense, friend, but I didn't come here to bond with you by sharing feelings and picking out sweaters. I need you heavily armed, bloodthirsty and pissed off."

Hollis continues his window shopping, chatting along the way. "Did you think you could just stumble into my yard misty-eyed, spewing flowering sentiment about your kid and I would gladly dive face-first into a sausage grinder? For you?"

"Yeah. I did."

"Do you completely understand my profession?"

"You kill people."

They pass an ice skating rink. Hollis shakes his head in frustration and thinks to himself, *Nobody gets my job. They think they know from watching movies and playing video games. 'Ooooh, look how cool it is to be a contract killer.' The hell with it. Just suffer the fools . . . can't kill them all.*

Hollis takes a deep breath and attempts to explain. "I'm a highly-skilled professional. I research everything. Nothing is a surprise. I monitor daily patterns. Wait. Watch. Plan. I take out targets from a hundred yards away. The goal is to work without the target, or anybody else, knowing what happened. I only go messy if a client wants to send a message, but that's an additional charge. My skill set is—"

"Calculated murder. Are you forgetting who you're talking to here?"

"It's what I do. What I don't do is kick in doors, spraying bullets like some entry-level cowboy who just jerked off to *The Fast and the Furious.*"

"What are you willing to do?"

Hollis takes a moment to ponder that while checking out the

display case of one of those places with the big-ass cookies. He makes a decision while surveying the buffet and says, "I will arm you. I will arm you well. I will show you basic tactical weapons scenarios, fundamental close-quarters techniques."

Not what Remo had in mind, but it's better than his other options, which all end with him cut to pieces and his remains spread like fertilizer.

Hollis continues. "I'll assist in developing some basic situational defense plans." He pauses to chat up a cute cookie cashier. "Just one. Chocolate chip, please." He turns to Remo. "You want a cookie?"

Remo feels more like throwing up again. Hollis takes the cookie from the cashier. He moves on through the mall, smiling the whole time like a three-year-old getting a big treat. Remo is forced to catch up, and attempts to get the conversation back on track. "Well. I mean, thank you, of course, but I was hoping you might pitch in."

"Go to the cops then." Hollis bites into his cookie. Soooo good.

Remo snaps, "You know damn well I can't. They hate me too. And, oh yeah, I threw a case and stole stolen money."

"You'll be alive."

"Disbarred, unemployable, in jail."

"Maybe your son is better off without you. You think of that?"

That stings. A verbal foot to the junk. The truth is a painful thing. He has thought about that and, sadly, the boy may be better off that way in the long run. Remo pulls a large envelope from his tattered suit jacket, hands it to Hollis and says, "In there is a DVD and a copy of my will. If this doesn't go my way, please give these to Anna. The DVD is for Sean."

Hollis takes the envelope with a nod, no reason to discuss it further. He's had to sit Jenny down and show her the "worst case scenario" box he has put together. Except Hollis's box contains

Swiss bank account access codes, a 9mm, passports, and approximately twenty large in cash.

"I'm the only one who can stop these guys," says Remo. "They've already dodged jail and the cops once."

Hollis gets it, but wants to make sure Remo gets him. "I've got a family, too. I've made my offer. Your call."

Remo has no play here, no leverage. There never was any. It's not a place Remo is accustomed to. He nods in agreement; he'll take what he can get at this point. Hollis nods as well, a silent agreement between two people who are the best at what they do. Up until today, however, Hollis has only taken advantage of Remo's skills, and Hollis knows it.

Next stop, Home Depot.

Remo feels like he's touching all the bases of the suburban diamond; golf community, Chili's, the mall, and now Home Depot. Perhaps they'll pull through somewhere for a diet cherry limeade and catch a dance recital. Hollis searches an aisle packed with a thousand nails and shit. Remo pushes a cart behind him.

Hollis takes the opportunity to begin his lessons and clarify some finer points of their arrangement. "That fantasy you're having of me swooping in like Han Solo . . . not realistic."

Remo snorts. "You were cooler when you had balls."

Hollis tosses him a high-powered nail gun.

Mattress Giant is destination two.

Remo follows Hollis with no idea why they are here. Hollis sucks down a diet cherry limeade as he checks the quality of various mattresses. Hollis bounces on one in particular, checks the specs on the tag. Not all mattresses are created equal, and his assessment has nothing to with the spine. He's looking for a mattress with the ability to stop, or at least slow down, a shit-load of bullets.

He flags down a dork of a sales guy. Wide as he is tall, probably been to Comic-Con ten times, and not the one in San Diego. Fuck that noise. San Diego has become all about the money, all about Hollywood's full-on rape of what was once pure. No sir, the true fanboys attend the New York City version of the pop culture event.

Hollis asks Remo, "How many downstairs windows at this place?"

"I don't know, ten maybe."

Hollis tells the sales guy, "Give me twelve of these." The sales dork has never been happier in his life; he hit his monthly nut with one customer. More *LOTR* figurines await him. He almost glides off.

"I can't turn you into Special Forces in a few hours. You ever even fired a weapon?"

"Used to get drunk in high school, shoot beer bottles with a deer rifle by the creek. Oh yeah, I shot out a window not long ago."

"Motivated Mashburn brothers might be slightly more challenging."

CHAPTER TWENTY-FOUR

DUTCH AND FERRIS enter Remo's apartment. They find Chicken Wing hogtied on the floor with the electrical cords. His face is swollen, still pulsing from being busted up by Remo.

Ferris snickers, "Such a tough guy."

"Fuck you piece of shit fuck-face cock sucker—"

Dutch cuts in, "Get him up."

Ferris goes to his little brother's aid.

Dutch leans over Chicken Wing, looking him over. "You think this behavior somewhat dampens the element of surprise?"

"In his defense, Lester fucked that up," Ferris chimes in. With Ferris's assistance, Chicken Wing begins the process of pulling free from the cords.

He fires back with a face-saving, "And I fucked Lester up."

"You're lucky Remo didn't bounce to the cops," says Ferris.

"Remo tried to run away," whines Chicken Wing, getting more and more defensive.

"And?" prompts Dutch.

"And I tuned him up."

Ferris raise his eyebrows. "Yeah, looks like you showed him good."

If looks could kill, Ferris would have ninety-seven bullets in his brother by now. Chicken Wing, finally getting loose from the cords, tackles Ferris to the floor. They go at it as homicidal brothers will do. Every third or fourth punch lands, a stray foot here and there. They're pretty rough-and-tumble dudes, capable of taking a beating as well as dishing one out.

Dutch lets it go on for a while; they need to get it all out. He looks to a clock and decides that's enough. "Stop." They pull away from each other immediately, as if Dutch was their father with a belt. "If he hasn't gone to the cops by now, he won't. He has too much to lose. We just have to adjust our plans." He turns to Ferris. "We still got safe passage?"

Ferris shrugs. “If we can afford the freight out of town.”

“Then nothing changes. Get our money, make Remo wish he'd never been born, and take a long holiday.” Dutch looks around the luxury apartment. “Tear the place apart. Find out where he is. He’s going somewhere he feels safe. Rather not wait for his invite.”

Dutch looks around, taking in the digs where Remo resides. He thinks of his last residence. The closet. The dog pen. The 10 x 6 Rikers condo he lived in during his little stay in shit-town U.S.A.

He reflects on that first night when Rudy tried to fuck him. Literally. Rudy must have had some daddy issues—or a thing for older men—considering Dutch was at least twenty years older than the boy. Dutch remembers hating himself for choking Rudy to death, after taking out one of his eyes. Not out of some remorse for taking the life of one of God's creatures. Please. Dutch hated the idea that this sick fuck probably liked being choked like that... until he died, of course.

That time in Rikers was all made possible by one man: Remo. Now Dutch stands in this gorgeous apartment where Remo eats, sleeps, shits and fucks. Probably fucks pretty women at will. Probably lounges around watching the tube in his underwear, never knowing the fear that comes from the ever-present possibility of gang rape. Remo probably ate well, not knowing anxious moments in a chow line. Those moments of checking your blindside for some bitch who wants to show the yard how hard he is by taking down Dutch Mashburn.

No, pretty sure none of that was an issue here for Remo.

If it wasn't clear before, it's crystal clear now—Dutch fucking hates Remo Cobb.

The younger Mashburn brothers, having been given their orders, are ripping through the place, scavenging like wild bears looking for good eats. Kitchen drawers get thrown, dumped. Dishes spin like Frisbees into earth tone walls and shatter, pieces falling to the floor. Chicken Wing tosses the king size mattress aside, as Ferris digs in the dresser without regard for the fine oak finish.

Dutch watches his brothers as he calmly pores over Remo's office desk for something that will help. Let those guys do the heavy lifting. He digs through files, checks some random business cards—mostly massage parlors—some random strippers' cell numbers, and a Subway punch card. He opens a drawer, finding a stack of bills. Flipping through them, he finds a few utility bills with an East Hampton address in Remo's name.

Compares them against Remo's other bills.

Dutch smiles on the inside—smiling on the outside is for women, fags and children. He turns to a laptop on Remo's desk, pulling up Google Maps. He enters the starting and destination addresses. A nice blue line shows the way. Those prison workshops are good for something.

He calls out to his brothers. "Got him."

THEY'RE GOING TO EAT ME ALIVE

PART IV

CHAPTER TWENTY-FIVE

THE POUNDING SOUND of relentless gunfire rattles and echoes in the background.

Remo and Hollis stand over a table sprawling with guns, guns, and more guns. It's a jaw-dropping buffet of firepower. Remo is excited with a mutated form of boyish glee. Hollis looks like he's buying toothpaste.

"I need an AK, right?"

"No," Hollis replies without even looking at Remo.

"I'd like an AK."

"You'll only hurt yourself. Give me two of those, Terry."

Terry, an old war-torn strap of beef jerky, is the proud proprietor of "Click and Pow," a haven for gun enthusiasts and anyone else who likes firepower. He grunts with every move he struggles to make. The years have been tough on Terry. He hands over two shiny 9mm Sig Sauers.

Hollis calls out items like ordering at a bakery. "One of those." Terry moves down the rack behind the counter. "Stock?"

Hollis thinks. "Pistol grip. And one of those."

Remo has no idea what's going on.

At the outdoor tactical course, Hollis walks alongside Remo

through the close-quarters course designed to simulate interior combat. Hollis thinks it's a poor simulation of what it's like to be boxed in with multiple murderers. That's impossible to simulate, but it's the best they've got.

Fake walls that form fake rooms and fake hallways do provide reasonably good practice for entering and clearing rooms in a way the average person might actually find themselves forced to do. The simulation uses human-shaped targets that pop out at you without warning. Some are children with lollipops, others are masked men with .45s. They keep the targets somewhat racially nondescript so as not to offend anyone who has a profiling bug up their ass.

Remo is equipped with a pistol grip Mossberg 12-gauge shotgun.

A target jumps out.

Remo fires.

The force of the blast causes the shotgun to fly from Remo's hands, skidding across the dirt floor in a dust cloud. "Fucking shit!" Remo shakes his hands violently, trying to get feeling back in them.

Hollis steps up, holding a custom-made swivel sling he got from Terry. He picks up the shotgun then pulls out a pair of strategically-padded tactical gloves with the fingers cut off.

Remo is starting to panic as he says, "There's no way. Might as well do it myself." Only half-kidding, Remo pulls the Sig from his hip, trying to jam it in his mouth. Hollis disarms Remo effortlessly, stopping him as easily as he would his two-year-old with a butter knife.

"I'm completely fucked, right? Fucked."

Hollis gives him a calming look, a look from someone who knows a little something about the art of click and pow. He attaches the strap to the shotgun and pulls the sling over Remo's head and shoulder, essentially turning the shotgun into a purse.

The shotgun hangs down by Remo's side for easy access, but doesn't leave his body.

Hollis helps Remo slip the tactical gloves—gloves specially designed for gunplay—over his pampered, manicured hands. Hollis and his buddies would guzzle beer after a successful job and make fun of people who needed these things, but now he realizes they have their place, and that place is on Remo's little bitch hands.

Hollis speaks with an even, calculated tone, not wanting to either scare or bullshit Remo. "These guys have been violent since birth. They have a huge advantage in the categories of 'balls' and 'killing.'"

"Still not helping, Hollis."

"You have home-field advantage and better tools." He points to the cardboard "bad guy."

"Look what you did to the target."

The shotgun blast sprayed the target from navel to fore- head. If it were a real person—a Mashburn—he'd be smoking a turd in hell right now.

Hollis taps the shotgun that now hangs by Remo's side. "This is a Mossberg 12-gauge gas-operated semi-automatic shotgun. Perfect for close quarters. Point and fire. Can't miss."

Remo looks at the mangled target. Starts to calm down a bit.

Hollis speaks in level tones, coaching, and teaching, working to build Remo up; trying to make him a good enough killer to survive this. "Try it again with the sling. Feel the weight, get comfortable with the sound and the recoil."

Remo grabs the grip, giving an uneasy nod. Hollis gives a wave to someone who works the course, starts moving alongside Remo again.

They round a corner. Remo scans the area with his Mossberg; it's clear. They push through an open door.

A target pops out. Remo fires. Target gets blown completely to shit. The shotgun flies from Remo's grip again, but only swings down to around his belt. Another target pops out. Remo is able to grab the shotgun from his side, comes up blasting again. Not seamless, but better.

Remo glances to Hollis. *Fine? Maybe. Okay?*

A sliver of hope.

CHAPTER TWENTY-SIX

LESTER STILL CAN'T BELIEVE how easy it was to find Remo's home address. Ask a few polite questions here and there, add in a few mouse clicks on the right websites, and what to do you know?

You can find anybody.

He gives the door a knock. He rubs his Bible while he waits, caressing the leather. He looks down, checking out his clothes. His escape-from-the-hospital garb. Sure, he's a former killer, thief, and convict, but as a newly reformed man of God, he's not pleased about running around NYC in a plain t-shirt and shitty sweatpants.

No answer at the door. He gives it another knock, pressing his ear to the door, angling for a listen inside.

Nothing.

Lester checks the hall, making sure there are no pain-in-the-ass innocents watching. He turns the knob; to his surprise, it's unlocked. He steps into the apartment, not surprised that it's a ransacked disaster. It doesn't take a criminal mastermind to deduct that Dutch and his bros were here. The place is ripped to shreds, not a single square-inch untouched. He knows it's probably useless, but he scans the place for Remo anyway, just in case he's bleeding out on the floor somewhere. There's no way Dutch would leave him here even remotely alive, but you've got to check all the boxes. He figures while he's here he might as well see if there are any items he can use on his mission of mercy. Lester enters the long runway of a closet, finding Remo's impressive wardrobe. He and Remo are not exactly the same size, but close enough. Fishing through the tailored garments, he comes across a nice navy blue button-down with some Italian dude's name on the tag. He tries on a couple of pairs of pants, finally finding a pair that will work for him. Nice cut, fine cloth. He completes the outfit with a pair of designer shoes with rubber soles.

At the top of the closet he spies a medium sized suitcase with rollers. He stuffs it with more clothes and slips his prized Bible between some pants and socks to keep it safe. He makes a quick stop in the bathroom and checks behind the shower curtain. No Remo. Lester takes the opportunity to take a swipe at his teeth by squeezing out some toothpaste on his finger.

Rinse. Spit. He rolls the suitcase into the kitchen. There's not much, but he finds a few non-perishable items: a can of soup, some crackers. They might get him through in a pinch. Lester helps himself to the loose change sitting in a large bowl on the counter. A set of culinary knives rests on the kitchen island in a wooden block. Lester inspects them, knowing that he will more than likely need something more than his hands and faith to stop the motherfucking Mashburn brothers. He slides the largest knife of the set out, revealing a massive butcher knife.

He slips the knife into the front pocket of the suitcase and closes the zipper. He'd prefer to keep it in hand, but knows he can't walk around NYC holding a butcher knife. He dodges the debris littered everywhere as he rolls the suitcase through the living room. The suitcase stops rolling. Leaning down, Lester notices the back wheels of the suitcase are hung up on Remo's baseball bat. Lester picks up the Louisville Slugger. Again, may fill a need down the road.

Lester gives the place another once over. He's come a long way. There has to be something here to tell him where to go. The Lord brought him here. No way his journey has ended with this. Seeing nothing, his heart sinks.

Poor, lost little Remo.

He rolls his new suitcase, packed with fresh clothes and weapons, toward the door. New items added to his meager collection of earthly belongings. Turning back, he gives the place one last look.

His eyes stop.

Remo's laptop. The screen is dark, but the little glowing green light indicates it's powered up. Lester flicks the mouse.

The screen lights up.

It still has the Google map to the Hamptons pulled up. Lester studies it, then scans the desk. Next to the laptop are the bills Dutch found.

Lester hits print.

CHAPTER TWENTY-SEVEN

FERRIS DRIVES. In the passenger seat, Dutch loads a crudely sawed-off shotgun. Chicken Wing's in the back, checking his .357 and sharpening a hunting knife—the one he keeps on his ankle for up-close-and-personal work. These are not the polished, tactically sound weapons of professionally-trained killers. These are the tools of men who were schooled in the violence of broken homes, poor neighborhoods, and shitty role models.

Something is obviously bothering Ferris. He's been running through possible scenarios concerning the death-match they are headed into. This is what Ferris does. Chicken Wing jumps without looking, and Ferris thinks. He wants to look at all the angles. No matter how crude the goal, he wants to be smart. There's something they haven't considered.

"We sure he's alone?"

There's silence in the van, as even Chicken Wing gives the question its due. Chicken Wing answers with a tone of impulsive wisdom. "Of course. Everybody hates the prick."

"Lester tried to help him, even after Remo put him in jail. I'm just saying, we don't know," explains Ferris. Dutch thinks. Chicken Wing doesn't bother with thought anymore. He tried it on for size; it didn't fit. He just wants blood and becomes a difficult little boy if he doesn't get it. On the other side of the spectrum, Dutch knows the answers to most of life's questions are usually somewhere in the middle. The correct answer to a situation is rarely balls-out one way or the other. Nine times out of ten it doesn't come down to "do nothing" or "murder every fucking thing moving." That's the yin and yang of Dutch's world: Ferris and Chicken Wing's dueling philosophies. Sometimes one of them alone does hold the correct course of action, but in this case Dutch feels down the middle is the call. There's too much at stake here for left wing/right wing (or Chicken Wing) partisan bickering. Dutch gives his ruling. “Make some calls. Find some local sluggers looking for fast work.”

CHAPTER TWENTY-EIGHT

EAST HAMPTON. Gorgeous homes sprawled on the coast of New York.

Vacation homes of the fortunate. Remo's second home. His den for meditation, his little hideaway and fuck shack. It lies in an area where the homes sit just off the water.

Great places to escape life for a while.

It's a quaint, two-story Victorian home with a sprawling, covered porch that wraps around the house. The backyard runs right up to the sand and water. A line of thick trees surrounds the front yard, secluding it from even the possibility of pain-in-the-balls neighbors looking on.

Hollis's Lexus SUV is parked in the circular driveway, two kids' car seats strapped in the backseat. Even a certified badass has to transport the kids.

In the distance, a repetitive chunking sound causes a dull echo to seep from the house. Inside the vacation home, Hollis works a high-powered nail gun. Remo helps by holding long straps of roofing material in place. They use it to secure one of the recently purchased mattresses in front of a window. Defense measures are in full effect. The other windows already have mattresses secured snugly in place.

Hollis looks around, inspecting his work. It's not bad. Not perfect, and it would never hold up in a military theater, but for a brief firefight among friends...it'll do. Hollis tells Remo, "You're all set upstairs, too." He gives a reassuring nod as he keeps working, surveying and planning for the upcoming attack on the house. Remo follows him like a child, watching everything and soaking up every word. Hollis knocks on a living room pillar, then another as he continues his inspection of every square inch of the home. Your average home inspection doesn't include a walk-through to assess the possibility of a battle with psychopaths.

Perhaps they should.

Hollis keeps scanning, spot-checking his work while consulting with Remo. "Don't worry about running out of bullets. I've got you stocked with enough ammo to invade Connecticut." He goes back to the middle pillar, giving it a hard shove, then tells Remo, "If you get boxed in down here and need cover, use this one. It's a support beam, it can take some hits."

In spite of all Remo's faults, he's not without gratitude, he's just miserable at expressing it. In his line of work, hell his life in general, "please" and "thank you" are not words he uses often. If he uses them at all, it's to manipulate the piss out of someone. Genuine appreciation is tough. Nevertheless, Remo tries by saying, "Hey man, I just—"

Hollis cuts him off. "Remember. Shoot and do not hesitate."

"Hollis—"

"You've probably got twenty, thirty minutes tops before the cops come swarming in."

"Can I say something?"

Hollis keeps checking points off his list without pausing for Remo to speak. "Oh yeah, wait until after I've left and call the Mashburns in."

"Hollis!"

Hollis stops the battle plan run-through and turns to face Remo. Hollis has perfected a way of looking at people that gives them nothing. He projects neither sympathy nor kind- ness, neither hate nor disdain. It is simply something undefined.

Remo hates Hollis's undefined face, but continues all the same. "You didn't have to help me." He starts to pace, playing with the shotgun sling, picking at it like a young girl would pull at an uncomfortable Sunday school dress. Completely uneasy with this sort of talk, he looks down at his shoes. "Most people in your position wouldn't piss on me if I was on fire, but you put aside all our baggage and I just want to tell you . . ."

He pauses.

How the hell do people talk like this all the time?

Feelings spewing all over the fucking place. However, he realizes he does actually feel better by saying it out loud. The weight is starting to lift; he's thanking Hollis and he means it.

It's a start.

He feels the warmth of contentment spread throughout him as he comes to grips with this revelation, this borderline sense of pride he's feeling from this little slice of self-growth. He's almost beaming as he completes this grand moment of thanks. He looks up to find...

Hollis is gone.

Remo blinks, spins around. Hollis has left the building. Remo finishes his thought out loud anyway. "Thanks."

The reality of his situation begins to creep back. The Mashburn brothers situation. The contentment and warmth are gone. Remo resumes his frantic pacing.

Outside the vacation hideaway, a van rolls up. The bad men are here. The worst case scenario has arrived.

The Mashburns exit the van. Scan the area. Check the Google map. Check their weapons. They're just down the street from the gates of Remo's property. Trees surround the gate and the nearby area. No words are spoken between the brothers, only a singular purpose between them: get their hard earned money and kill Remo . . . in no particular order.

Chicken Wing buzzes with a manic energy.

Ferris is cautious and controlled, but ready for violence at the flick of a switch.

Dutch has the confidence that comes from being a successful, lifelong madman.

They make a determined, single-minded march, descending upon Remo like the messengers of death they are.

Inside the house, Remo is wearing out the floor, pacing like an expecting father. He's almost pulling his hair from his scalp, thoughts burning him down from the inside out. Nothing can prepare you for what is coming for Remo. He looks at the checklist Hollis prepared for him, just in case Remo freaked out and forgot. Remo pooh-poohed the very thought when Hollis suggested actually putting pen to paper and writing out a list, but Hollis was right. Remo has started to freak out and has forgotten everything, including #1.

Calm the fuck down. Remo moves on to #2. He straps on his Kevlar vest and takes a deep breath, trying to find his center, to find a place in his head where he can function. He knows there's no way out of this.

Remo checks the window. The sun is starting to set. He knows it's time to call them. Fights it, but it's time. He pulls his cell, ready to dial.

It rings before he gets the chance.

Remo drops the phone, picking it up on the second bounce. Heart in his throat, he answers.

"Great place, Remo." Dutch's voice digs a hole in Remo. Shell-shocked, panic strips Remo to the bone. He flies up the stairs with all the grace of a pregnant yak.

He skids across the hardwood in the second-floor bedroom on his knees, stumble-rolling into position in front of the sniper rifle perched at the ready. His breath is heavy, partly from running upstairs, mostly from the knowledge there are armed whackos in his yard.

He presses his eye to the scope, views the perfectly manicured yard. It's empty. Still. Peaceful. It's almost as if the plush grass is waiting for war as well.

Remo grabs his cell. He takes a big swallow, saliva hard to come by. "What do we do now?"

"Well, maybe you come outside with the money."

"It's nice in here, Dutch," says the shaky Remo.

Along the tree line, Dutch has taken cover with a good view of the front of the house. This isn't the first time Dutch has stormed a house, though usually it's a crappy apartment or some half-ass meth shack in the middle of nowhere. This is a significant step up in tax brackets, but the same school of thought applies. *This is a good spot,* thinks Dutch, *for now.*

Ferris waits a few trees over, soaking up the details of the house, listening to and observing the landscape, trying to calculate the best play here.

Chicken Wing is yet a few more trees down, Glock in one hand, .357 in the other. These are the times that make the man tick.

Ferris gives a look to Dutch, almost telepathic communication firing between the two brothers. It's clear they don't like any of this. Chicken Wing just wants to hurt someone

Dutch replies, "Why don't you come outside? Haven't seen you in years."

Remo just stares through the scope, completely frozen. He heard Dutch's words, but his focus is on not pissing himself. He knows coroner's reports, what they read and how they circulate around the city

The deceased pissed his pants before he was killed. Not how a man would prefer to be remembered.

CHAPTER TWENTY-NINE

REMO HAS the rifle's sight plastered so tight it's nearly become part of his eye.

Sweat beads, verging on pouring. Heart pounds hard against his ribs. He moves the rifle from side to side, trying to keep aim on them, trying to keep up with the Mashburn brothers. They change positions, improve their positions, constantly moving behind trees, making it damn difficult on Remo.

Not the Mashburns' first rodeo.

Outside, Dutch's eyes alternate between his brothers and the house, trying to get a read on the situation. Where's Remo's head? What does he have going on inside that house? Aside from the language, Dutch uses the tone he would take with his mother as he speaks to Remo. "Just toss out the fucking money and we can go grab a beer down the road. Have a laugh about all this."

Remo knows that's not so subtle a code for he's a dead man no matter what. Replies, "Sorry, I've got a thing later."

There's a crunch of brush behind Dutch. He turns. The local sluggers have arrived. Dutch would smile if he believed in it. Dutch is fairly confident the advantage is now firmly in his favor, no matter what that asshole has waiting in that house. Dutch tells

Remo, "Tell you what. I'm going to send Chicken Wing to the front door, and if you're less than hospitable . . ."

Remo adjusts his sight. His eyes bulge as he sees Chicken Wing step from the tree line. Remo takes a little bit of pride in the fact that his handiwork has left Chicken Wing looking like he got his ass kicked by a bad man.

He exhales deeply, says back to Dutch, "If he's cool, I'm cool."

Chicken Wing takes a couple of steps forward from the tree line into the front yard, toward the front porch of the house. He looks around; the coast is clear. Gun in each hand, he begins walking, moving out onto the lush front lawn.

From his second-floor vantage point, Remo's finger tickles the trigger, fumbles a bit. He looks away from the scope, wipes the sweat away and then goes back again. Thinks, *I really should shoot this guy*.

It's harder than he thought.

Chicken Wing keeps walking at a steady pace. Not in a rush, but not a slow walk either. The steady, determined march of a killer. His mind dances with the heart-warming thought of blowing Remo's face off. It's a beautiful day. He looks back to Dutch, gives a toothy grin and a shrug. This is going to be sooo damn easy.

A loud crack of gunfire sounds out.

The single shot explodes into Chicken Wing's shoulder. The impact spins him around, but he remains on his feet. The Glock flies from his hand, landing softly in the grass. The shot echoes, followed by eerie quiet.

The whole world seems to disappear.

Complete shock rips through Chicken Wing. This doesn't happen. For a fraction of a second, he thinks, *so this is what it feels like.* Fucking sucks to get shot. This is as close to empathy as Chicken Wing has been or ever will be. His shoulder seeps, a bloody mess.

Dutch and Ferris's surprise quickly turns into hostility. Their brother is a headache and an unquestionable fuck-up, but he's their brother and they take exception to anyone shooting one of their own.

Up in his second-floor perch, Remo can't find his breath. He can't believe he did it. "Holy shit!" He's excited, taken back to that little kid at the carnival in Cut and Shoot, Texas, who knocked over milk jugs with a baseball.

Remo finally understands what all the fuss was about, why so many of his clients take pleasure in shooting the people who piss them off. So this is what it feels like to shoot an asshole. Pretty fucking sweet.

Chicken Wing holds his shoulder with his .357 hand, twirling in circles in the front yard, trying to shake loose the pain. Sucks in through his teeth with hard, short breaths. Blood slips and spills through his fingers. Seeing red, he releases an inhuman war cry from deep inside. Wounded animals sound more pleasant than this. The hollow, angst- dripping wail cuts through the air. The streaming, blistering sound that pours out from Chicken Wing is the stuff of mythological beasts.

Remo looks on from above, boyish excitement fading. It's become abundantly clear he has simply awoken a sleeping, psychopathic giant.

Fuck.

Chicken Wing's wail continues as Dutch and Ferris spill out from the trees. They don't hesitate as they open up heavy suppression fire. Sporadic waves of bullets pelt the second floor. Dutch wraps Chicken Wing up in his arms, moving him along while blasting away.

Remo's eyes snap wide open. Bullets whizz by him, popping and zipping through the walls and windows. He pulls himself back up to the rifle, shielding his eyes from the flying glass. Before he can get his eye to the scope, he sees through the blown out window three hard-hitting, tougher-than-leather thugs spill from the trees armed for war, storming toward the house. Big as linebackers, armed like a SWAT team, they fall in behind the Mashburns. Remo hasn't seen these cats before, doesn't know who they are. This new, united army thunders headlong toward the front porch, big guns and bad attitudes at the ready.

Remo's world slips into slow motion—they say that happens during car wrecks and times of personal danger. His thoughts explode, compress, then explode again.

This is how his dad died. This is how he's going to die. This is how his son will remember him, pissing himself before dying a horrible death.

What was it Hollis had told him before he left?

Oh yeah, something about shooting and not hesitating. Remo forgets the scope and just starts firing, ripping off shots as fast as he can, shrapnel, glass and bits of house bouncing around him.

Bullets churn up the front lawn by the fistful. Most of the shots miss the impending doom coming Remo's way, not even slowing them down to a jog. Then, one lucky shot lands. A leg is knocked out from under one beefy thug. Actually, it's almost blown off at the knee. Remo takes the time to aim and fires another while the thug's a stationary target. The high-velocity round plugs the thug in the chest, sending him hard to the grass.

Remo doesn't waste time on the victory. Spit flies from his mouth as he releases his own battle cry, firing with all he has until...

Click. Click.

Fumbling for a reload, he hears sounds from downstairs. Beating. Kicking. Ramming at the front door. Glass smashes, the sound muffled by a pillow-top mattress covering the window. Remo scrambles to the stairs, shotgun in its tactical sling bouncing like a badass handbag. He takes the stairs as if they weren't there. About two steps from the bottom, the front door takes a blast from a 12-gauge, the door knob flying past Remo's head. Another shotgun blast takes out the deadbolt. A thug punches through, door flinging open to reveal a wall of a man brandishing an AR-15. He looks like a badass right up until the point he's met by a shotgun blast from Remo. Just like it did at the range, the Mossberg flies from Remo's hand, but stays close thanks to the sling. He scrambles to get control of it again. The thug falls back through the door onto the porch, body flops like a side of beef. Ferris and Dutch watch the body land, blood pouring from the wounds. Dutch motions for Ferris to go around back with the remaining local muscle.

Before leaving, Ferris gives Chicken Wing an *Are you okay?* glance. Chicken Wing waves him off. Not the time to baby the man. Rage erases all the pain of his blown out shoulder. Ferris and the thug take off around the house.

Dutch and Chicken Wing take positions on either side of the front door, Dutch calling out to Remo. "You are a cocksucker. That much is certain."

Remo listens as he rushes to the Hollis-approved pillar for cover.

Remo barks, "Aren't we way past name calling, cunt?"

At the back of the house, Ferris and the thug round the corner into the small backyard overlooking the beach. The sun setting over the water would be gorgeous if not for the bloodthirsty criminals and hostile gunplay. Remo keeps his head on a swivel. He can make out movement on the porch, also the shadows moving around back. He knows they're coming at him from all angles.

"You're boxed in Remo. Give this up," calls out Dutch.

Remo's breath shortens, blood pressure elevates. The walls are closing in.

Dutch keeps up the talk. "All we want is the money."

"It's all in nickels now. That okay?" Remo smirks to himself. It's good he can still crack wise.

Dutch shakes his head with a wry grin. Funny man, that Remo. Chicken Wing is not amused. His ravaged shoulder has robbed him of his sense of humor.

Dutch replies, "We're going to come in there, and we are

going to kill you. Or, we can make one last deal. Give us the money . . ."

Remo is all ears.

"And I won't chop up Sean."

Remo's blood turns to ice. He closes his eyes tight, wishing he hadn't just heard his son's name come from Dutch's mouth. A bad situation just blew past worse on its way to unimaginable.

Dutch keeps working him. "What did you think? We wouldn't find out? That's cute. I haven't seen him myself, but I hear he's a real nice-looking boy. Why don't you come on out? You decline and everybody dies in a very nasty way."

Remo can only listen. He has no angle to play.

"How about I drag you along so you can watch what I do to the boy? That's a better idea. Yeah, I like that. Whatcha think, counselor? Sound like a plan?" Dutch talks like a man who knows he's holding every card in the deck. Except the money card, which Remo stole from him.

Ferris and the thug stand at the back, guns ready to blast open the door. Ferris has to strain, but he can hear Dutch from the front porch. He holds tight, waiting for some kind of sign from Dutch.

Dutch checks his .357, wondering which bullet will be the one to blow Remo's brains out. "Your call, counselor."

Remo's lost, thoughts racing around his head at breakneck speed.

How did it get to this?

What have I done?

I've put Sean and Anna in danger.

What do I fucking do now?

"Remo? You still with us, buddy?" Dutch is giving the performance of a lifetime. "You can save your boy's life right here and now. I hate the countdown drama, but I guess there's a reason it happens. I'm giving you a three count. If you don't come out, well, ya know, the math on this is simple."

Remo closes his eyes and listens to Dutch countdown.

"One..."

Ferris and the thug listen with bated breath from the back of the house. "Two..."

Weapons up.

Fingers on triggers.

Chicken Wing is so ready, .357 itching to go off.

"Remo? There's not gonna be a two and a half."

Remo takes a deep breath. The only thought in his head is for his son, his Sean. Probably should have been his only thought for years. Not that Sean wasn't on Remo's mind, but it wasn't enough. Even Remo knows that.

What Dutch doesn't know is that before he threatened Sean, Remo may have lost focus. If this was only about Remo, he may have slipped up, fucked up. But somehow, when it's about something bigger than Remo, he finds a new level of concentration. Caring about someone more than you do about yourself does that to a man. Remo has been forced to think beyond himself, beyond his future, his career, his wealth. He has been forced to understand that what happens here is going to affect something he truly cares about. Even if he could give a fuck or less about himself, he cares about Sean. Remo may have made a mistake without Dutch's careless threat, but the only mistake made here today was by Dutch.

He dragged Remo's boy into this, that asshole, and that fucking changes everything.

Remo's eyes snap open. He exhales with a focus he's not known before today. He grips the shotgun tight. The tension is wire tight. Everything that happens from now on, happens really fucking fast.

"Three."

CHAPTER THIRTY

THE HINGES BLOW off the back door.

Remo whips around, leveling his shotgun. The back door is kicked loose from the frame, sending it slamming and sliding along the kitchen tile. In the same moment, a crash sounds from a front window as Chicken Wing dives through, hurling himself into the mattress, ripping free the nails holding it in place. Chicken Wing rides the mattress down to the hardwood floor. As he slides with the pillow-top mattress, he manages to come up with his .357 pounding.

Chunks fly off the pillar Remo hides behind.

Ferris and the thug flood the room and Remo opens fire, trying to hold them back. Ferris and the thug dive in two different directions as they scramble for cover.

Dutch steps through the front door. Remo is now completely surrounded.

Chicken Wing continues laying down hammering fire, and Remo spins from the pillar, letting loose a shotgun blast that misses wide.

Chicken Wing's shot doesn't miss.

His bullets cut the air, Remo catching a bullet in the center of his Kevlar vest. It spins him like a top. Better than being shot without a vest, but still hurts like a bitch. Another shot from Chicken Wing hits Remo's arm and pain explodes, burns throughout his body. His teeth grind as white-hot pain spreads from his wounded arm. His shotgun falls to his side.

Ferris comes up behind Remo, sawed-off at the ready. Remo collapses to a knee holding his arm, still trying to find some air for his lungs after taking that bullet to the vest. As he falls to his knees, Chicken Wing unleashes a reckless barrage of .357 fire while screaming like a banshee. His uncontrolled blasts miss Remo as he thrashes from side to side.

They don't miss everyone, however.

.357 slugs tag Ferris in the chest and face tearing thick, fleshly ice cream scoop style wounds.

Chicken Wing's .357 clicks empty.

Ferris tumbles dead in a heap to the hardwood. What's left of his head bounces off the floor.

Chicken Wing stops cold. Stunned. *I just killed my brother.* That reality grabs hold, twists and strangles the youngest Mashburn's simple little head. Remo sees an opening. Now or never. Summoning every fragment of strength he has left, ignoring the greatest pain he's ever felt in his painless life, he pulls his battered body up. His feet slide and scramble to find traction as he flees down a hallway. Dutch unleashes a flurry of fire, blasts churning up the floor behind Remo's scampering feet. The thug follows suit, blasting away.

A blood trail winds behind Remo as he slips into a room at the end of the hall. He slams the door behind him, bullets tearing through the walls. Remo stands in his home office, a room lined with thick books, random office supplies, and other lawyer shit. A large, solid oak desk sits at the back of the spacious room, a long window along the far wall. Remo locks the door, wedging a chair quickly under the knob.

He regards the blood pouring from his arm. No time to fuck

with it. He rushes to the heavy desk. With everything he has left in his tank, Remo pushes the desk over, toppling it to the floor. He slips down, taking cover behind it.

Back in the living room, Chicken Wing is a manic mess, his eyes flooded with tears of anger.

Chicken Wing screams silently as he holds what's left of his dead brother. His mouth is wide open, but nothing comes out. His face is a dark red, veins bulging and popping from his neck and forehead.

Dutch, cold and inhuman, allows Chicken Wing a second to grieve. That's it. He storms over, slapping the taste from Chicken Wing's mouth as he barks new orders. "Not now. Pull it in." Chicken Wing pushes the tears down, controls his breathing. Dutch loads the .357, shoves it back in Chicken Wing's hand, saying, "Everything inside you right now, use it. Feed on it...and kill him."

Huddled behind the office desk, Remo reloads the Mossberg with his good arm. Pumps. Grits his teeth. The sound of something wicked plowing down the hallway shakes him to the core.

A guttural scream from Chicken Wing gains power as he stampedes down the hallway. Stripped of all human traits, the primeval Chicken Wing slams his body into the door with all that he is, zero regard for his shoulder wound. He plunges his full weight into the door repeatedly, bloody smears from his arm's hard contact with the wood covering the door. He steps back to get a running start and lands a solid foot to the door.

Another. Then another, and another.

CHAPTER THIRTY-ONE

As Hollis drives his Lexus out of town, his mind is in a twist. He turns on the radio, flipping the stations. Turns it off. He hates himself. It's all over his face. He hates himself for even thinking about Remo. "Fuck him. Fuck. Him." Hollis knows he's almost out of this; the city limits are in his sight. He's done enough for that prick. More than anybody ever should, that much he knows. He tries the radio again.

Then.

Hollis spots a black Escalade with the windows blacked out and heavy tint. A gangster ride if ever there was one. It's completely out of place here. This isn't the kind of neighborhood where this type of pack would travel. Not without a reason. Not without a score, or a score to settle. He watches the Escalade pass by him. The driver's window is down and Hollis catches a glance at the passengers. A heavy-hitting crew of bad boys.

Hollis knows they can only be headed to one place. After they pass, Hollis takes a self-loathing pause. Takes that time to try and determine the weight of the situation, understand what is actually happening here. Those guys are going to Remo's. Of course they are. If Remo is even still alive, he won't be for long. Hollis starts beating the steering wheel. "Dammit. Fuck. Shit."

The Lexus does a screaming U-turn.

CHAPTER THIRTY-TWO

DUTCH TEARS up the stairs to the second floor in search of his money. In the distance he can hear Chicken Wing going nuts, working that office door like a champ. Dutch pours through closets, behind furniture.

Nothing. A new feeling for Dutch—fear. Where's the money? In the office, Remo is curled in a fetal position behind the pushed-over desk. He can only watch and wait as the door is battered by Chicken Wing's relentless attack.

It's almost open. Won't be long now. Remo's mind spins, trying to find a strategy. He pokes his head up for a look. *Smash!*

The thug flies through the window, squeezing off a couple of rounds in mid-air. Remo drops behind the desk. In the same instant, Chicken Wing finally busts through the door, his bloodlust in hyper drive. The thug lays down fire, holding Remo down behind the desk. Overwhelming fire rains down. Remo is forced to stay down, pinned behind the overturned desk.

Chicken Wing runs wildly toward the desk, dropping the .357 and pulling his knife along the way. He wants the feeling of tearing, of ripping, of cutting Remo's flesh by hand. He wants to slow-bleed this fucker.

From behind the desk, Remo hears Chicken Wing's footsteps rumbling towards him. They're slightly muted by the thug's pounding fire, but the rolling thunder of Storm Chicken Wing is coming.

Chicken Wing leaps, looking to go over the desk, looking to land his knife into Remo's skull.

Remo pops up at the last second, getting a point-blank blast off with the Mossberg. The shot catches Chicken Wing in mid-air.

Almost cuts the kid in half.

As chunks of Chicken Wing's corpse land with thick, wet sounds, his knife jams deep into Remo's thigh. Remo cries out in agony. The thug keeps firing, shots hitting way too close to the thrashing Remo. Remo manages to turn his shotgun in the general direction of the thug. Knows his shot doesn't have to be perfect—just point and shoot. He rattles off two fast blasts, blowing the thug's upper body into pulpy bits.

Remo knows this is far from over. He pulls the knife from his thigh—to say it's painful is the understatement of the year—clinching his teeth, his face draining of color.

Oh shit.

He's bleeding badly, almost every part of his body something to be concerned about. Thinks he could pass out.

Gotta make a move.

Dutch whips around the corner, firing with double-fisted .357s.

Remo drops to his belly, managing to fire two blasts which push Dutch out of the room, back into the hallway. Dutch takes cover behind the door. This is taking its toll on him as well.

In the distance, the sounds of sirens wail.

Dutch knows he doesn't have much time. He calls out to Remo. "Hear that? Cops are coming."

Nothing from Remo.

Dutch makes a silent two count and spins, coming hard through the door firing.

Remo is long gone.

He did leave behind Dutch's almost-cut-in-two dead brother and the bloody remains of a hired thug for Dutch's viewing pleasure. Dutch has learned the valuable trait of compartmentalizing his emotions. It's a skill that will get a man through a lot of bad days inside, if you can master it without completely checking out of your head. Dutch will, at some point, grieve for the loss of his brothers.

Now is not the time for that shit. He eyes the blown out window to his left.

It's starting to get dark outside. Remo is running on fumes as he drags his beaten, barely functioning body through the woods. He takes cover, propping himself behind a tree where he has a good line of sight on the house. Remo readies his shotgun. He'll wait for Dutch to come out, end this damn thing.

One way or another.

A decent plan, all things considered. Then he notices a dead, heavily tattooed body with a single, clean bullet wound between its eyes. Way too skilled for Remo.

Who the hell?

He looks around, sees another similar body. Same perfect wound.

The guys from the Escalade.

Of course, Remo doesn't know this. Crunching footsteps sound behind him. Remo turns, readies his shotgun.

Movement from a tree not far from him.

Remo reacts without thought, doesn't have time to process who it is before he pulls the trigger. His shotgun blast hits Hollis, sending him flying backward to the ground.

No! No!

Sure he's killed Hollis, Remo dives to his side. *Please no, not this.* Remo can't compartmentalize this the way Dutch can. Hollis is a friend, of sorts, and this is a cross that Remo cannot bear. Hollis's face is cut up, a few stray hits in the shoulders and belly.

Peppered buckshot shows all over his Banana Republic wrinkle-free Oxford.

However, there is no blood to speak of.

Through the holes in the shirt, shades of black show, giving the sight of the Kevlar vest Hollis is wearing. Wounded, but he'll make it. Remo breathes again.

Hollis spits out, "You are such a fucking asshole."

"Shit. Sorry."

Hollis's eyes go wide. Remo doesn't have time to turn before Dutch is on them. He rams Remo at full speed, the force knocking Remo clear of Hollis. Dutch beats on Remo while screaming out, "Where's my money? Where?!"

"Gave it away," says Remo, taking a solid punch to face.

"Where is it?"

"Look at you. Big, bad man. Listen good. Your money is with the family members of the people you and your piece-of-shit brothers murdered."

Something in Dutch comes unhinged.

Remo spits out a tooth, saying, "It's gone baby, gone."

Dutch's rage has been building for a lifetime. Taking care of his brothers when nobody else would. Years inside a cell.

Time waiting for a prize that was never even there. Someone must pay the full freight for these heavy burdens. Dutch unleashes punches backed by a primal animal furry. Face, neck, ear—doesn't matter where they land to Dutch as long as they inflect pain. His veins pop. Spit flies.

Remo is pinned down, his only option to lie there and take the beating.

Dutch feels around for something, anything, to finish the job. He fingers find a large rock. He raises it above his head, ready to crush Remo's skull.

Dutch can taste it, the moment he's obsessed about. Remo's death is in sight.

Remo can only watch, motionless, as the rock rises above him, casting a shadow across his face.

Hollis pulls his 9mm, shifting to get a clear shot. It's not there.

The solid clunk of a baseball bat connects with the side of Dutch's skull.

Lester stands over Dutch, bat in hand.

Remo watches Dutch's body wilt to the dirt, blood spreading out around his head. Sitting up, Remo attempts the impossible task of comprehending the last hour of his life.

Hollis holds his gun on Lester. Lester grips the bat, not about to stand-down. Remo can't help but notice: *did he steal my fucking clothes?* He jumps up yelling, standing between Lester and Hollis.

"No, Hollis, I know him. Lester, stand-down. You did good. You saved me. God's proud."

Lester's expression remains hard, war-ready. Not a single facial muscle moves. Hollis keeps his gun on Lester; it's what he does.

The sirens are very close now.

Remo continues talking Lester down. "We've gotta go, man."

On the ground, an indecipherable grunt comes from Dutch. Hard to believe it, coming from a man like Dutch, but it's a whimper of sorts. A dying man looking for some kind of mercy in his final minutes.

Lester nods to Remo, then flashes a cold set of eyes to Hollis before turning his attention to Dutch.

His former partner in crime. Current object of anger. Up until now, Lester has done a fine job of keeping his violent tendencies in check, stuffing his old self down under the surface where it wouldn't cause harm. Like all pressure that builds, it has to be released. Lester's under pressure, and his violence needs to be released, regardless of his newly found path of the righteous.

Lester remembers the Preacher Man saying, "Personal growth is a work in progress."

He'll ask for forgiveness later.

Lester lifts the bat high over his head and rains down a frenzy of brutal swings to every inch of Dutch's body. Bones crunch as wood lands over and over. He pulls the butcher knife from behind his back. Grabbing a fistful of Dutch's hair, he attacks his neck, sawing away with the massive carving blade.

Tendons pops. Blood gurgles. The sickening mix of sight and sound is too much for Remo.

It reminds Hollis of a night he spent in Singapore many years ago.

Remo and Hollis rush through the woods, the sirens continuing to get louder as they move out of the trees toward Hollis's Lexus. Remo wants to look back at Lester, but doesn't.

He knows that some things can't be unseen.

Pale. Bleeding.

CHAPTER THIRTY-THREE

PISSED, but working through it.

Hollis is laid out in the passenger seat while Remo drives away from his house in the tranquil Hamptons. A stream of police and emergency vehicles blow past them, headed the opposite way. Remo watches as they pass, checking his rearview.

Hollis is a pro, always. Even with the annoying little flesh wounds, he manages to disassemble his gun in record time and with absolute precision. He tears away from his carved up vest and dumps all of it in a black, Hefty lawn & leaf bag.

Remo alternates between looking at the road and Hollis, admiring his work and curious about what's next. His wounds throb, but Remo thinks it would be in bad taste to bitch to Hollis about the pain. You know, considering that he shot the man.

They haven't said a word to each other since Hollis called him an asshole. Remo can't take it and decides to break the silence. "Dude—"

"Shut up." Hollis isn't interested.

Now Hollis truly hates himself for going back. He could be watching the Golf Channel right now, or perhaps playing with the kids while nursing a cocktail. Worst-case scenario, he'd be attempting to talk the wife into an evening blowjob. The possibilities were endless.

Now, however, his possibilities are somewhat limited. He pulls his cell and scrolls through his contacts. To Remo's surprise, Hollis speaks in perfect Mandarin to whoever is on the phone. The conversation takes less than twenty seconds, but it's damn impressive. Hollis hangs up and barks to Remo, "Give me those." He motions to Remo's equipment. Remo pulls off the sling and vest, doesn't ask questions about the Mandarin.

Hollis stuffs all of Remo's hardware in the bag as he speaks. "You drop me off a couple of blocks from Dr. Wu's house." Motions to his wounds. "I'll take care of this, and you can go fuck yourself."

Remo bites his tongue. Again, given the fact he's the one who shot Hollis, he should just take it. Of course, that's not a truly viable option for a guy like Remo. He reflects on the day's events as he says, "Not to be a dick, but you had a gun."

"I was going to shoot him, but your whackadoo buddy showed up and—"

"You took your sweet-ass time as that animal beat the piss outta me."

Hollis winces and continues packing everything in the bag. "Shut. Up."

"Pretty sure you did it on purpose, that's all." Rolling silence.

No eye contact. "Fucking hate you," mutters Hollis. Complete silence the rest of the way.

CRAZY, CRAZY HEART

PART V

CHAPTER THIRTY-FOUR

CHILDREN AND PARENTS are playing their hearts out, soaking up family time at Gramercy Park on a gorgeous Saturday evening. Anna and Sean sit on a bench, waiting for Remo. Sean, every bit the wide-eyed boy who can't sit still, looks like any child would if they were waiting for Santa or the Easter Bunny or meeting their dad for the first time. He bounces with anxious energy while his mom tries her best not to look how she feels. She doesn't like this, but she holds it together for her boy. There's a gasp, followed by a low murmur spreading through the park. The low hum starts to grow as whatever's going on gets closer to Anna and Sean.

"Oh my God."

"Is he okay?"

The commotion finally catches Anna and Sean's attention.

Turning, they see the cause. Remo.

A bloodied mess, he's somehow pulling himself through the park. He's barely able to walk, a staggered crawl of sorts. He stumbles through the park without regard for his body or others' for that matter.

Puts a foot in the middle of picnic blankets, in plates of food.

A sandwich squirts mustard as his heel plants in the middle of the rye.

He interrupts games of catch. Knocks over a girl texting. He resembles the grace and style of a zombie with epilepsy.

It hurts to watch him move, powering through despite every cell of his body yelping in agony.

Anna stares. *What to Expect When You're Expecting* doesn't cover these moments in life. "Remo?" she asks, covering her son's eyes as Remo makes it over to them.

He stands up as straight as he can. Adjusts his shirt. Sways a bit. Although he looks like he's been touring the bad side of hell, he's glad to be there at the park. It pains him, but he gets out, "Hey, guys..."

Then falls face first to the ground like a broken pile of bones.

CHAPTER THIRTY-FIVE

AN EYE FIGHTS TO OPEN. It's a real struggle, but the lid finally gives way with a slight crack of healing skin. The lid flickers slowly, reluctantly, as it finds its way to a semblance of normal. It begins blinking rapidly, working overtime to find moisture and feed an eye that feels like you could strike a match across it.

Remo's lone good eye dances around, checking out the room he's found himself in. Doesn't recognize it, but coming to in a strange room has happened before.

It's a stark, clean place. Not a bar, a whorehouse, or even a lady's strange apartment with cats and shit. Most importantly, he's woken up and not found himself in a coffin.

It's a box of a room that's trying very hard to be a livable space. Not much furniture to speak of, bland dime-store paintings hanging on the walls. The sun peaks through heavy curtains, cutting shafts of light across the white tile floor. Remo is laid out in a hospital bed. Struggling to come around, he smacks his lips.

Feels like a cat shit in there. He forces his lids to remain open. He thinks about the cartoons he watched as a kid where they used toothpicks to hold their eyes open, lids crashing down, snapping them in two. Up until now that seemed silly and unrealistic to Remo. Today, however, it's possible.

Tubes and machinery are attached to various points of his body. Something to the left drips. Another thing to the right dings softly every so often while numbers bounce across a screen. He's held together with tape, gauze and a little bit of hope, but he's alive. Pain fires through every inch of him as he sits up, trying damn hard to regain his senses.

His voice cracks as he says, "That was a horrible idea." He stops short, realizing he's not alone. There is a person staring at him. A little person.

Sean.

Perched at the foot of his near-deathbed is his son. A perfect little face rests in tiny hands, propped up by scrawny elbows. Sean has found a safe distance from which to watch, but he's close enough and curious as hell. The young boy gives a slight, apprehensive wave. Remo winces through the pain, but returns the gesture.

A hopeful splinter in time for Remo.

Remo turns, noticing that along the wall is a line of other folks who were waiting for him to wake up as well.

Folks just dying to chat with Remo.

Detective Harris leans against the doorframe, along with a pack of his fellow officers, all looking like they would like nothing more than to rip Remo's face from his skull and nail it to the wall. ADA Leslie has wedged herself in a corner of the room, sharing a similar expression.

Anna sits in an uncomfortable chair. She could care less about Remo. She's a ball of nerves as she watches Sean. *What was I thinking? I knew somehow something like this would happen. Fucking Remo.*

Detective Harris breaks the ice. "Remo. Would love a word."

Remo puts up a hand, asking for a moment. He wants to say something to Sean. No idea what, but he's gone through some serious trouble to have this opportunity, and wants to have this moment.

He starts to say something, stops. Thinks better of whatever was about to come out. Anna watches with the same level of apprehension she'd have watching a dog trying to cross a highway. Sean sits with his little heart beating fast in anticipation. Remo knows there's no way to say what he needs to say, what Sean deserves to hear, so he opts for silence instead.

Sean lets him off the hook by asking, "Who are you?"

Remo smiles, the closest thing to genuine happiness you will ever see out of him.

"One asshole."

They share a big smile as an infectious giggle rolls out of Sean.

EPILOGUE

THE PLAN? Simple.

Murder multiple motherfuckers, save one asshole.

That was the strategy of one Lester Ellis, a former criminal, former wheelman, current man of the Lord.

Mission of mercy complete.

Lester walks alone on a back strip of country road about 20 miles outside of Syracuse. A light rain falls over him. *Feels nice,* he thinks. He rolls his suitcase down the road, still dressed to impress with the clothes he borrowed from Remo's closet. The wrapped grip of the Louisville Slugger pokes out the top, zipper as close to closed as it can get around it.

Now what? thinks Lester. The Mashburns are gone baby, gone, and Remo is safe from them and their wicked ways. He hopes Remo has found a better path, at least better than the one he was on.

He has to. After all the hell he endured. Can a man not change after surviving an experience like that? There's another question that truly troubles Lester. It plays with his brain like child picking at a scab.

Who was that man Remo was with?

That man with the gun.

That man seemed to carry a heavy burden as well. A different burden than Remo for sure, but the weight of the burden that man is hauling around can't be ignored. The kind you've been carrying so long you don't even know it's there—the worst kind.

It was in his eyes.

Lester has learned how to get a lot from someone in a short amount of time. Just let him see the eyes; it's all in a man's eyes. It's really all you have to go with when a man has a gun on you, and that man would have shot Lester dead. That much Lester knows. The man Remo called Hollis has killed before, that's for damn sure.

Is Remo truly safe while he's keeping company with a man like that?

Lester thinks not.

Lester turns his suitcase around, heading back in the direction he came from. Back toward NYC. He needs to make sure. As he turns, the suitcase tips off balance, toppling over to the road. He bends down, taking a moment to adjust its contents. Unzipping the bag, he moves the clothes around, trying to get the balance back in working order. He opens a bulging black trash bag nestled among the clothes.

Inside the bag, Lester grabs a fistful of hair, shifting Dutch's head.

Once satisfied, he zips the suitcase up again and continues rolling down his path.

His newly chosen plan.

A SAMPLE FROM REMO WENT DOWN

Book 2 in the Remo Cobb Series

The water in the pool is cold as shit.

You'd think an indoor pool would be heated for fuck's sake. Before jumping in, Remo stripped bare-ass naked. His Kiton suit is balled up in a chair with his dress socks stuffed into the toes of his slick, black Salvatore Ferragamos.

He feels his balls shrivel up into sad raisin-like nibblets.

He hears the screams from the old ladies.

Their water aerobics class has been suddenly cut short by a former big-time attorney diving into their pool with his dork swinging. Well, at the very least, it gives a slight sway.

Remo thrusts his arms in and out as hard as he can. Cutting the water. Swimming deeper and deeper like a madman to the bottom. Desperately trying to reach the floor of the deep end.

He's got a Phillips screwdriver in one hand and it's hurting his ability to carve through the water like the aqua god he knows he is, but there's no other way to do this fucking thing. He curses himself for setting up the emergency pack like this. It seemed like genius at the time. Of course, at the time he was hammered out of his skull and on the downside of a two-week bender with a couple of women from Australia who dealt in the white powder game.

Good times.

After much effort, he reaches the drain cover. Manages to get one screw off before having to make a panic swim back up for air. He takes a big suck of oxygen, hears someone call him an *asshole*, then plunges back down toward the drain. This time he gets all the screws, pulls off the cover, and removes a gold key.

Exploding to the surface, Remo gasps hard, sucking in as much air as he can. He thinks he's going to die. He hasn't held his breath that long since he went down on that muscle-bound Russian lady during the Cunnilingus Incident of 2007.

Holding on to the side of the pool, he can hear the insults and squawking of his new pool friends. As he pulls himself out of the pool, he realizes he's now standing in front of a pack of very angry older women. Dripping. Naked. He says nothing, allowing silence to fill the room.

He lets them stare at his member.

He simply holds his hand out, waiting.

One woman smiles big, blows him a kiss and tosses him a towel.

Remo cracks a grin, snatching the towel from the air with a snap and a wink.

Remo's still the goods, baby.

WANT TO KNOW WHAT HAPPENS NEXT WITH REMO & FRIENDS? TURN THE PAGE!

Click or tap below to...

GET REMO WENT DOWN NOW!

OR

(And this is much smarter...)

Get all four books in the Remo Cobb series plus a bonus and save a few bucks...

GET THE REMO COBB BOOKS 1-4 PLUS A BONUS NOVELLA

Thank you for reading.

Mike McCrary

ALSO BY MIKE MCCRARY

The Remo Cobb Series

Remo Went Rogue #1

Remo Went Down #2

Remo Went Wild #3

Remo Went Off #4

The Steady Teddy Series

Steady Trouble

Steady Madness (Coming Soon)

Standalone Books

Genuinely Dangerous

Getting Ugly

FOLLOW MIKE ON BOOKBUB

Be the first to know when Mike McCrary's next book is available!

You can now follow Mike on BookBub to receive new release alerts. Just tap or click below and then tap or click Follow.
BOOKBUB - Follow Mike

I've been a waiter, screenwriter, a securities trader, dishwasher, bartender, investment analyst and an unpaid Hollywood intern. I've quit corporate America, come back, been fired, been promoted, been fired again. Currently, I write stories about questionable people who make questionable decisions.

Always great to hear from you. Please follow or contact me at:

www.mikemccrary.com
mccrarynews@mikemccrary.com

ACKNOWLEDGMENTS

You can't do a damn thing alone, so I'd like to thank the people who gave me help and hope during this little fun and self-loathing writing life.

First, thanks to Elmore Leonard, Don Winslow, Stephen King, Chuck Palahniuk, Duane Swierczynski, Charlie Huston and Dennis Lehane. You don't know me, but thank you for what you do. Thanks, in no particular order, to the following writers, badasses, good dudes and Book Gods: Blake Crouch, Tom Pitts, Allan Guthrie, Joe Clifford, John Rector, Peter Farris and Johnny Shaw. Thank you for talking books and the publishing world with me, even if you didn't know you were doing it.

Big, massive, sloppy love to the good folks at MXN Entertainment (Michelle Knudsen and Mason Novick) for never wavering in their help and support over the years, thank you doesn't cover it, man. Michelle, thank you for the greatest note ever, "Why did you kill Lester? He's the best part."

Love and appreciation to my family and friends who have put up with me and my bullshit—you know who are. Thanks to Mom and Dad for not selling me for medical experiments, and last but not least, thank you to my amazing family. You have endured and embraced me during my bitter, cranky, moody and (let's just say it) dark days. For that and for everything, every day. I love you.

Cover by J. T. Lindroos

Made in the USA
Las Vegas, NV
29 August 2021